X

Closed Doors

ALSO BY LISA O'DONNELL

The Death of Bees

Closed
Doors

A NOVEL

Lisa O'Donnell

HARPER

www.harpercollins.com

HarperCollins books may be purchased for educational, business, or sales promotional use. For information, please e-mail the Special Markets Department at SPsales@harpercollins.com.

Originally published in Great Britain in 2013 by William Heinemann, an imprint of Random House.

FIRST U.S. EDITION

Designed by Michael P. Correy

Library of Congress Cataloging-in-Publication Data has been applied for.

ISBN 978-0-06-227189-1

14 15 16 17 18   OV/RRD   10 9 8 7 6 5 4 3 2 1

To my sister, Helen

one

I'm not spying on Mrs. Connor, I only watch her dance because her windows are so low and I can reach. All the houses
have low windows where we live because all the houses are the
same. A sort of sandy orange color, except Alice McFadden
says they're peach and I don't know the first thing about color
because I'm a boy.

"Michael Murray, I hate you, you don't know anything
about anything and your fly is always open." I look down when
she says this in case my fly is open but it's not open and then
she goes "Ha, made you look" and skips away to find someone
to tell. I want to punch her in the face for it and if she was a
boy, then that's what I'd do. I'd smack her so hard. I wonder
if I can punch her on the arm next time I see her but I know
she'll go bawling to her brother and so I shout after her and
call her a "cow" but then she goes bawling to my ma who calls
me in and makes me apologize to Alice and her fake tears. She
loves getting people in trouble, that Alice. I don't know how
Marianne Cameron can stand her. They hang around together
all the time, mostly singing and dancing. They're practicing
for their talent show and who knows when that will be. They're
always going on about it. I bet it never happens. They've had
posters taped on every lamppost in Barone for months and

months. They're mostly drawn by Marianne, who's brilliant at art, although Alice drew the one next to Mrs. Connor's house. It's rubbish. They say they're going to have the concert in the car park and are having auditions, but some of the girls on the street don't want to sing because Marianne is singing and they can't dance either because Marianne is doing some Highland dancing and some ballet. Tracey Stewart and her mad ginger hair says it isn't fair Marianne is doing all the good stuff, so Marianne says Tracey can make the costumes and Fiona Brown with the longest legs in the whole wide world is going to help her. They're also doing some backing vocals on a few of Marianne's songs with Alice. Paul MacDonald is going to dribble his soccer ball for everyone to see because Paul thinks he's great at soccer, but he's not as good as me. I'm going to do keepy-uppies on my knee. Fat Ralph wants to flip over, but because the car park is made of concrete, Marianne says he'll kill himself and it won't be safe, so he's going to jump up and down with an invisible guitar or something like that. I'm looking forward to hearing Marianne sing, she sings really well. Alice doesn't. Alice can't do anything Marianne can do. Marianne is brilliant. Her hair is nice and she looks clean. Alice looks dirty and so I call her Dirty Alice, but not to her face, behind her back. It always makes people laugh when I say it, except Marianne, she doesn't laugh, not one bit.

"That McFadden girl needs a good bath and a comb put through her hair," says Ma.

"Poor man," whispers Granny and then crosses herself because Dirty Alice's ma died, leaving her with her big brother and a father who never opens the curtains.

"Can't move for the grief and there's Luke left to do everything for the girl and him only fourteen years of age," says Ma.

"I saw him taking two big bags of shopping into the house last week," Granny says. "It's no way to live," she adds.

"Know you're lucky," Ma spits at me, even though she's always sending me to the shops for this thing and that thing and sometimes for women's things. That's what Da called them.

"It's a disgrace. Get them yourself. Don't be embarrassing the boy. Hide them under your jacket, son."

And that's what I did. I don't mind really. I do all sorts for my ma.

"Angel baby," she'll say, "go do your ma a wee favor." Angel baby is her special name for me. It also means I'll get some money out of it for sweets. I love this name.

All the houses on Barone sit high on a hill and overlook the sea and the town where we live. Ma says people in other parts of the world pay huge fortunes for beautiful views and stretches of sand.

"Good luck to them," says Da.

Ma loves where we live and like Da and Granny she has lived here her whole life. She doesn't want to go anywhere else, not even when she could have. Everyone says Ma is very smart and could have gone to university or something like it, but she was too in love with my da and mad for the island, even though people here gossip all the time and want to know all your business. It makes my granny crazy, even though she gossips all the time and wants to know everyone's business.

"You can watch the ferry going in and out from the harbor all day long," says Ma. "Who wouldn't want a view like that?" she tells my da.

Ma says we did good getting a house on Barone Hill and it was brilliant of Margaret Thatcher to build them for us. That's when Da tells her to "Shut the 'F' up" because Da hates Margaret Thatcher and because she didn't build them anyway. A big fight always happens when he says the F-word, and words like "beer," "bitch," "dole," "stupid," "unemployment," and "lazy arse" go flying around the kitchen until a door slams and locks all the words away. Da quickly grabs his coat and goes to the pub after a fight like this and Granny says that's why he started the fight in the first place, so he can get out of the house and drink.

"He'll be home later stinking of beer and eating chips," says Granny. "You see if he won't."

Later I sneak out of bed to share the chips. Da is always pleased to see me. He does smell of beer but I don't care because the chips are so good. He'll switch on the telly and we'll watch Barry Norman telling us about all the great films we can see when we go to the mainland in Glasgow, except no one ever goes to the mainland in my house. If you want to see a movie with Al Pacino or Indiana Jones in Rothesay you have to get it on pirate tapes from Knobby Doyle, but you also need a video recorder and we don't have one of them. Da says he can borrow one, maybe at Christmas, and that gets me excited.

"Why do you hate the prime minister, Da?" I ask him.

"She only cares for rich people," he says.

"Ma likes her and she's not rich."

"Ma likes the house, Michael, and she wants to buy it with my old man's money and pretend she's rich."

"It's a nice house. I like it."

"Let me tell you something about Margaret Thatcher. If

she gets away with it she'll have us paying for everything. Education, son. Medicine. Now she wants me to buy the house and make all her problems my problems. I wouldn't waste one penny of my father's money buying this place. Your mother's a madwoman. The place would blow away in a storm."

"Is there going to be a storm, Da?" I ask.

"No, son," he sighs. He lets me finish the chips first before he packs me off to bed. He's like that, my da.

two

Mrs. Connor looks like Blondie, but then all the ladies look like Blondie round here, except Katie Calderwood, she wants to be Suzi Quatro and has her hair all spiky and wears a leather jacket. Ma says Katie Calderwood looks like a man but she would never say that to her face.

"She's built like a brick shithouse," says Granny. "She'd smack you in the gob."

This makes Granny and Ma laugh until they're falling about the place.

"And what about that father of hers?"

Ma and Granny exchange looks.

"What about him?" Da says from behind his paper.

"You know fine well," says Granny to Da, but Da doesn't know "fine well" and tells her so.

"He's a willy woofter," says Granny.

"Away you go," says Da.

"He definitely curls his hair," says Ma.

"The man has a natural kink. He has two children for gawd's sake."

Da is getting annoyed. He hates the gossiping of Ma and Granny.

"You're only defending him 'cause you drink with him," says Ma.

"I'm defending him because he is a man like I am. He drinks pints, has babies, and works in construction, that's no place for a homosexual," says Da.

"What's a homosexual, Da?" I ask.

Da looks uncomfortable, so do Ma and Granny. This means I'm going to get tossed from the room or lied to. I get tossed from the room.

I take my soccer ball to the garden and think of Mrs. Connor, who mostly wears a dressing gown when she's dancing, except when she goes down the road to the shops, she dresses up then and wears a stripy skintight dress or a pair of satin trousers like Olivia Newton-John from *Grease*. She looks paler in the sunlight, but she's still Mrs. Connor and looks nice.

"It's a shame her husband left her," Da says. "He must have been mad."

"She looks like a prostitute," says Ma.

"And drinks like a fish," says Granny.

Da tells Granny to be quiet and mind her business, but Granny can't. She loves to talk about other people and their business, it's her favorite thing in the whole world, and so she waits till Da is out of the room and calls Mrs. Connor a slut. Then she whispers a story to Ma. I can't hear them but Ma nods and tuts and sighs.

"Disgusting," Ma says to Granny.

Granny nods. "I told you. A regular wee hussy," spits Granny.

Ma sees to the laundry. I really hate our laundry. It always stinks of cigarettes because Granny and Ma smoke like chimneys. I bet my teachers think I smoke I stink so badly.

"How many times do I have to tell you, Rosemary? I hate the smell of fags on my shirts. Can you not stop for five minutes, at least while you're doing the washing?" snaps Da.

"Why don't you do the washing?" Ma says and flings a vest at him.

"You're a couple of fishwives, you know that? You could spend all day in this kitchen smoking and talking shite about folk. It's a disgrace."

"Not all day. She has a job, remember?" Granny says.

Ma's a cleaner at my school. When we finish our adding and our writing she comes through the park with her leather handbag and gets to mopping up the mess. It's a big job because there's linoleum everywhere, but they have these huge machines with giant brushes to make the floors shiny and the next day when you're at school you can slide on them like an ice skater.

"Filthy little buggers they are," she tells Granny. "The crap I've cleaned up in that place, you wouldn't believe it. And don't get me started on the teachers' lounge. Now there's a shithole for you."

"Why? What's it like?"

"Fags squashed into teacups if you can believe it," says Ma.

"Dirty bitches," says Granny and shakes her head as if she's been told a million people have died in the yard.

"And the headmistress . . . let's just say I know the reason she's so bloody happy all the time." Ma tips her head back and pretends she's drinking something.

"No," says Granny in astonishment.

"Yes," says Ma.

When Ma's working, Granny makes the tea. Da hates Granny's stew. He complains and gags every time she makes it.

"You try cooking for four on what we're living on. You'll eat it and you'll like it," she says.

"Will I?" Da growls and puts the fork down. He fetches himself bread and jam instead. I'm not allowed the bread and jam. I have to eat the watery stew.

My granny rolls her eyes when Da gets like this and when he leaves the room she tells me he's a "moaning whining bastard who needs a job." She shouldn't say the B-word to me but she does anyway and then she crosses herself to make it all right with God. My da says Granny is a mixer and I'm not to listen to anything she says and since she's his ma he should know.

They mostly don't get on, my granny and da. She likes my ma better because they're women and because my granny doesn't like how my da has turned out in life, working on building sites and painting folks' houses. "It's a wee island," says Granny. "Only so many houses you can build and only so many you can paint."

"It's a developing community," says Da.

"Developing?" smirks Granny.

Da doesn't want to fight with her. He just pulls a face and sticks his head in his newspaper. Later he goes to Old Mrs. Thompson's house and paints her front room for thirty pounds.

"Spend it all on drink he will," says Granny, but he doesn't. He gives it all to my ma and this makes Granny happy and so she gives Da a wink. This makes Da pleased with himself and there is no fighting for a while.

Granny can be tough sometimes but she is a good helper around the house and would lay her life down for her family. This is what Ma says and Da agrees. Granny used to be a nurse but retired to enjoy her life with Grandpa Jake, but then Grandpa Jake died and Granny came to live with us. He had a heart attack and left Da all his money; it wasn't a lot of money but enough to make Granny hurt. Da said it was for the best because Granny is addicted to catalogues and Woolworths. He said she would have spent the money in a week and we need it for the future. He lets her live with us because she cried so much after Grandpa Jake died and wouldn't get out of bed.

Ma likes to have her stay with us. They talk all the time and Granny helps her in the house. Ma's an orphan. Granny told me but Da shook his head when she said this because Ma was a grown woman when her parents died.

"She's hardly Oliver Twist," says Da.

Ma's parents died when I was just a baby. Words like *orphan* scare me because it means you have no one. Granny says I'm not to worry. "You'll always have me in the event of a crisis, Michael."

Da laughs at this. He says my granny is right and will outlive us all. Ma thinks this isn't a nice thing to say and gives Da a right dirty look.

"Can you not take a joke, Rosemary?"

Ma ignores him and lights another cigarette. Da rustles his paper and shakes his head.

"Would you two just stop?" snaps Granny. And they do stop, but not in a nice way.

three

Everyone is playing Kick the Can. It's a great game. One team covers the can while the other team hides, then the other team comes out of hiding to try and kick the can without being caught and being sent to jail. The winner is the team who can kick the can without being tagged. It's my most favorite game in the whole wide world, except on Saturday when I catch Marianne and Paul MacDonald kissing next to Paul's da's garden shed with Dirty Alice keeping watch, except she isn't very good at keeping watch and lets me see. It makes me ill. They were crouching like frogs. Marianne wasn't even touching him but he was all over her. He had his hand on her shoulders and was right next to her face, while his other hand was holding on to her arm like he thought he might fall over or something. I would never have kissed her like that. I'd have given her a big hug or touched her hair. I hate Paul MacDonald for touching her and I hate Marianne Cameron for letting him near her.

It wasn't fair and so I go tell Marianne's da. This causes Marianne's da to go to Paul's da to make a big fuss. Paul's father isn't even bothered though and keeps nodding and shrugging his shoulders at Marianne's da, who is very thin and called Skinny Rab. I can't hear what they are saying but when they start to laugh and stuff I know no one cares Marianne and Paul have been kissing. Marianne hates me now and won't let me do keepy-uppies at her stupid talent show because even though Marianne's da and Paul's da were laughing, Marianne and Paul have to stop kissing now. Even the girls hate me because it's spoiled Marianne and Paul from being boyfriend and girlfriend. I'm glad though because it's got rid of the sick feeling I had in my stomach when Dirty Alice made me see them kissing. I hate Dirty Alice and I will punch her in the arm next time I see her.

four

I am woken from my bed and it's still nighttime. Everyone is talking at once, my ma is screaming and my granny is asking for God. I can hear my da but he doesn't sound quite like Da. He sounds like someone else. His voice is higher than usual and I wonder if the house is on fire. I put my slippers on and sneak downstairs, but I am heard on the step and Da is quick to the staircase.

"Michael, go back to bed," he says. His face is red and frightened. I don't like it one bit. I hear my ma crying and my granny whispering in the background; her words are soft, the kind you say to a child who has fallen.

"What's the matter, Da? Why is Ma crying?" I demand.

"Go to bed, Michael." He sounds desperate and wants to go back to the kitchen. He keeps looking at the door. There's something behind it and I'm not supposed to see.

"Please, Michael. Just go upstairs," he begs and then uses the wall to hold him up, like he thinks he might fall over or something.

Da never talks to me like this and so I go upstairs, but I let him know I'm not happy about it. Da watches me go. I can feel his eyes on me. He waits at the bottom of the stairs until he knows I am in my room and then he removes himself and

13

goes to the kitchen. The door is closed tight behind him. I wait for five minutes until a new commotion begins downstairs. It's like they can't stop themselves. I decide I've had enough and go downstairs. I am very careful to avoid the creaky step this time. I make it to the kitchen door and no one has heard me. I'm quite pleased with myself and lean against the door.

"You must have seen something. Think!" begs Granny.

"He has a gold chain on his wrist. It was heavy," cries Ma.

"What else?" says Da.

"He was tall," whispers Ma. "I don't remember anything else. It was dark. Oh God, he wouldn't let me go till he had a smoke." She starts to scream. Granny has to get her to calm down. She's probably worried about the neighbors. Granny is always worried about the neighbors.

"We have to call the police," says Da.

"No," cries Ma.

"What are you talking about?" says Granny. "There's a madman out there."

"No, Shirley," begs Ma. "I don't want people to know."

Granny and Da go quiet. Ma whispers something else through sobs and I can't hear anything.

"No," says Da. "You don't know what you're saying!"

"It's what I want. We'll say I fell. I won't go to the police. I won't. They'll say things about me. Terrible things. Oh God," Ma yells out. The crying continues and so much of it. I wonder what's wrong with her. Then Da tells Ma she shouldn't have been walking through the park at all. "If I've told you once, then I've told you a thousand times go down the high street. Why the hell would you walk through the park anyway? It's pitch black." I hear him cry like a baby. I haven't heard my da cry since John Lennon died and I must have made a noise because the next thing the door is suddenly ripped open and Da is standing there, his face wet with tears.

"What do you think you're doing?"

I look past him to Ma. Her face is bloody and Granny is holding her so tight I wonder if Ma can breathe.

"What happened to Ma?" I gasp. I want to go to her straightaway, but Da won't let me past him. "What's wrong, Ma?" I ask. Ma buries her head in Granny's chest. She can't even look at me.

That's when Granny tells me Ma has seen a flasher. Da gives Granny a terrible look as if she's said something mad.

"What's a flasher?" I ask.

"A pervert," Granny screams and grabs Ma tighter.

"Why is there all this blood, Da?" I ask. It's making me scared and I think I might cry.

"Ma fell over, son. She ran away from the bad man and then she fell, don't worry, son, away to bed now," says Da.

"That's right, Michael. This man flashed your ma and scared the life out of her, then she tripped and then she fell and . . ." Granny doesn't finish. She starts bawling her eyes out instead. "Take him upstairs," snaps Granny at Da.

"What about Ma?" I plead. "She's hurt. I want to stay with her, Da."

"Come on, son," says Da. He puts his hand on my shoulder and leads me from the kitchen all the way upstairs to my bedroom. Da sits me down on the bed. He tells me I'm not to say anything about the flasher.

"Why?" I ask.

"People might say things," says Da.

15

"What things?"

Da is running out of words and rubs at his forehead.

"I don't know," he whispers.

I worry he'll get upset again, but I still want to know about the blood and Ma and the flasher.

"Da?" I ask. "Tell me why we can't say anything."

"Because they might not believe there really was a flasher, Michael," whispers Da.

"But why?" I ask. Nothing makes sense to me. Nothing.

"For Christ's sake, Michael, just say Ma fell down the concrete stairs in front of our house, will you?" Da is getting mad, but I don't care. Everything feels wrong to me.

"But why? Should he not go to jail for flashing at Ma and making her fall like that?"

"No one is to know about the flasher. Do you understand, Michael?"

I still don't know what flashing is but I nod in agreement and promise not to tell. Then Da asks me to go to sleep. I agree to that too, although we both know the house is going to be awake all night and I'm right.

Later Da calls a taxi and takes Ma to the hospital. I know this because Ma is screaming she doesn't want to go. I watch them from Granny's window. Da has to hold Ma up. When he comes back a few hours later it's without Ma. I am desperate to know about Ma and sneak back downstairs. I know I'll get a hiding this time, but I don't care.

"Did she tell them?" says Granny.

Da shakes his head.

"Then what did she say?"

"Nothing. She can hardly open her mouth for God's

sake. . . . They think I did it, Ma, you should have seen the look Tommy Gordon gave me in the taxi, even the doctors think I did it. They asked me so many questions. I told them she fell down the stairs, but they weren't having any of it. The police took me down the station."

"You have to tell them the truth," gasps Granny.

"You heard her. She doesn't want it."

"She didn't know what she was saying, Brian, don't be stupid," says Granny.

"She made me promise, Ma. She said people would say all sorts about her. Maybe she's right. I don't know. You know them better than me."

"People would understand. This wasn't her fault," says Granny.

"Would you understand, Ma?"

"Of course I would. What do you take me for?"

"What about Bridie Forsyth?"

"Bridie Forsyth couldn't keep her knickers on and Peter Hughes is a good man who goes to chapel every Sunday. He's very good-looking. He wouldn't hurt a soul."

"You don't know the first thing about Peter Hughes. He's a fucking drunk and a mean one at that. No woman would make a thing like that up. She had to leave the fucking island with the gossiping."

"You know how Bridie was. She was looking for it, if you ask me!"

"And maybe that's what they'll say about Rosemary. She's terrified, Ma."

Granny is silenced. I wonder who Bridie Forsyth is and what it was she was looking for.

"You'd rather they thought you beat your wife to a pulp?"

"It's what Rosemary wants," he cries.

"And what do you want?" asks Granny.

"I want to kill the bastard," cries Da and then there's a banging on the table.

"A lot of good that will do now. We don't even know who he is," says Granny.

I've heard enough and go back to my room. In the morning I am full of questions. Granny folds laundry and Da looks tired. I ask him about flashing. He doesn't want to tell me. Neither does Granny. They want me to disappear with my soccer ball, but I don't. My ma has been flashed at and I want to know what it means. She's in the hospital with a sore face and a limp. She fell hard because of this flasher. I have a right to know what's going on and why I'm to tell everyone she fell on the stairs. Da gives in and tells me flashing is when a man shows a woman his willy and makes her afraid for her life, and so I hope Dirty Alice is flashed. I hate her more than anyone in the world. She's ruined my whole life because no one will talk to me or play keepy-uppies with me and now Paul MacDonald might fight me because I told on him for kissing Marianne. I don't want to fight Paul MacDonald, he's bigger than me. Paul MacDonald is bigger than everyone.

five

I listen at doors now. It's the only way to find out stuff. No one tells me anything.

When Ma comes home from the hospital she looks worse than she did before. Her face is like a balloon and she has stitches, some on her cheek and one above her lip.

I hear Da tell Granny the police can't touch him because Ma said he didn't hurt her, but the police don't believe her anyway. I know no one told them about the flasher.

"I'd be shamed," she says to Granny.

"If it was a different town," sighs Granny.

"But it's not!" snaps Da and goes back to his paper. I wonder if he's even reading it.

Things go very quiet at home for a while. No one listens to the radio and when I watch TV I have to keep the sound very low so as not to upset Ma. Da doesn't talk about Margaret Thatcher even though we might be going to war soon and everyone is talking about it at school. My teacher Mrs. Roy says we are the owners of the Falkland Islands and Argentina is trying to steal them from us. She says our prime minister will do what is right for the country because she is a great woman. Deirdra Smith yells "Boo" and calls the prime minister a "milk snatcher." No one knows what Deirdra is talking about and she is sent to the headmistress. When she comes back to class, Mrs. Roy makes her sit on her own and write lines. When I told my da what Mrs. Roy said and what Deirdra yelled he didn't say anything. Da doesn't care about Margaret Thatcher anymore. He doesn't even go to the pub on Sunday to play darts. Da loves darts.

Ma's been off work for a couple of weeks and Granny uses her medical experience to help her as much as she can. I think my granny must have been a good nurse. Anyway, when Tricia Law comes to visit her, Tricia gets the shock of her life because of all the stitches on Ma's face.

"That was some fall," Tricia says to Ma.

Granny offers Tricia a seat but she's secretly annoyed I let Tricia into the house at all, but Tricia has been to the house a thousand times to smoke and drink tea and I thought Ma would like to see her. Da looks like he's going to kill me. Ma looks like she's going to cry. I am sent out to play.

Eventually I see Tricia leave the house. She is going to work and will probably walk through the park to clean the school. I want to tell her about the flasher.

"Hey, Michael, come here a minute," she calls.

I put down the soccer ball and run to her. Tricia always has sweets and chewing gum in her purse. I like Tricia; she is my favorite friend of Ma's and is always laughing about this thing and that thing. She's fun to have around. I thought she might cheer Ma up, but she didn't.

"How's your da?" she says.

"Fine," I say back.

"Whereabouts did your ma fall?" she asks.

"On the stairs in front of the house," I say because we have hard stairs and that's what Da told me to say if anyone asks.

"Is that right?" she says. She takes some gum out of her purse. It's Juicy Fruit. I love Juicy Fruit. She gives me two pieces and a big smile. She takes out her cigarettes because she likes to smoke like Ma and Granny. Everyone likes to smoke round here and it drives me mad.

"You know you can come to me about anything funny going on, Michael?" she says. "I know your da likes his beer, but if he's ever shouting or making you or your ma scared you tell me, OK?"

I nod.

"See you later," she says. "And be a good boy for your ma."

I nod again and she walks away. She is going to clean the school and will probably take the shortcut through the park. I want to tell her she's in danger but I am too scared of Da and I am called in for my tea. I decide to ignore Granny's call and follow Tricia instead. It's still light out and maybe I can catch the flasher and everyone will be happy.

Tricia walks fast and it's hard to sneak behind her and not be caught. I know Granny and Da will kill me when I don't come in for my tea, but saving Tricia from a pervert and his dirty willy is more important.

Tricia smokes her cigarette as if nothing will happen to her and it won't because I am right behind her. I follow her all the way along Caledonia Walk and wait for her to turn into the park but that's not what happens; she meets Skinny Rab and they disappear into a dark place until they're giggling and laughing and having a good time in the bushes. They take a long time by the wood and eventually Skinny Rab comes out pulling at his fly. Tricia follows him and gives him a big kiss, then Tricia says good-bye and turns into Barone Road. She's not going through the park after all. Skinny Rab waves at her and goes home to Marianne and her ma. I go home to my house. I get a kick up the arse from Da and I'm sent to my room without any tea, but I don't care, I don't care about anything at all.

six

It's been well over a month now and Granny says Ma has to pull herself together. Granny says she has to get on with her life. Ma nods and gets out of bed, and then goes to the bathroom and everyone rolls their eyes to heaven. Da asks about the flasher every chance he gets.

"Try and remember something, anything. He's out there, Rosemary. He might hurt someone else. I don't want that on my conscience."

It makes Ma cry when he says this.

"I just want to get on with my life and forget," she says, or "You know how they are round here" or "Stop asking me that" or "I can't remember" or "What are you trying to say, Brian?" Mostly she says she can't remember. It drives Da wild. He banged a door once and put a dent in it. Granny went off her head and told him to calm down.

"You think this is helping?" screams Granny.

"I can't take it," he says. "The bastard is out there. He's walking around, Ma. I want him dead. I want him under this fist begging for his life."

"You think she doesn't?" yells Granny.

Da shames quickly. Granny usually knows what to say, not all the time but a lot of the time. Da grabs his coat.

"Where are you going?" says Granny.

"For a walk," growls Da.

"You won't find him, Brian. He's gone now," Granny tells him. Da still goes out, and Granny shakes her head and sighs. He won't be back until late and without chips, just the smell of fresh air from all his searching.

Ma has to have a bath every night and uses up all the hot water. She also makes Da sleep on the sofa, it's like she can't stand him sometimes. It drives everyone mad because it's not Da's fault, but no one says anything because of the flasher. Then Da starts asking Ma if she's OK, like all the time. It gets on her nerves after a while.

"Stop asking me that. I'm fine," she tells him.

"You're far from fine," says Da.

Granny says Ma should go back to work or people will start to wonder what's wrong with her. Da says Ma isn't ready. Ma says nothing. Granny says Da has to get a job or use some of Grandpa Jake's money then.

"We can't live on fresh air," says Granny.

"She's NOT ready," repeats Da and slaps his paper on the table.

"People will think we're keeping her prisoner or something. She's never out of the house," says Granny.

"I don't give a flying fuck what people think," says Da.

I know serious things are being said when the F-word is being used but no one throws me from the room. No one has thrown me from the room in a long time. They're so upset about the flasher they forget I'm standing there at all.

"Well, I do," screams Granny and slaps a tea cloth on the table. I feel bad for the table.

Ma sighs and tells them to stop fighting and agrees to go back to work. This makes Granny happy.

"It's for the best," says Granny.

"It's a mistake," says Da.

"Your ma's right. I need to move on," whispers Ma.

"But you're not ready, it's only just happened," yells Da.

"To who, Brian? To you?" yells Ma.

"To everyone in this house," snaps Da.

Everything goes still for a minute. Ma picks up some laundry.

"I'm only thinking of you," calms Da.

He puts his hand on Ma's shoulder. She wriggles away from him.

"Leave me be then," she says.

"You're doing the right thing, Rosemary. Put this behind you and get on with your life."

Da gives Granny the dirtiest look I've ever seen and storms off as usual. He's not welcome anyway. Ma and Granny are fed up with him and so am I. He's always angry or sad, noisy or quiet. It's hard to know with him these days. Ma wants to fold the laundry and Granny wants to make her terrible cake. I don't know what I want.

After the laundry is folded and Granny's sponge is baked, Granny suggests a walk down the town. I think this is a good idea. Ma's face is better and she can walk without limping. Da hates the whole thing.

"She needs some air about her," snaps Granny.

"She needs to rest," yells Da.

"Would you two stop talking about me as if I'm not here?" screams Ma.

My head is pounding with the three of them. Everyone yelling and slamming doors. It's a madhouse.

"I think a walk would do me good," agrees Ma, but in a whisper, as if she's not too sure.

"You don't have to do this," says Da.

Ma shrugs him away. She grabs for her coat and the whole family goes down the town. I get pocket money from Da, a whole fifty pence. I love him for that. Ma looks nervous, but Granny tells her to put a brave face on. Da tells her she'll be OK. Granny tells her no one knows anything and not to worry. Da tells me to keep my trap shut about the flasher. Then Granny says we should go to the Tartan Tea Room for a spot of lunch. I could burst with excitement. They do great milk shakes and serve the best scones. I think it's great Ma is getting out of the house.

We don't have a car and so we walk to town, but no one minds because it's a nice day.

Da walks next to Ma and Granny holds my hand, but I pull away. I don't want Granny holding my hand. Holding hands is what girls do with their mas. Da tries to take Ma's hand, but she doesn't want to hold hands either. She holds tight to her leather handbag instead. No one says much until we meet Mrs. Maitland coming from the chapel. Mrs. Maitland is always coming from the chapel, where she cleans things up and arranges flowers. Granny says she's sucking up to the priest to get a better place in heaven. Mrs. Maitland talks about this thing and that thing and everyone nods their head in agreement, but then she says Da should think about getting me baptized. Ma says "No" because her mother and father were Protestants.

This disappoints Granny because she's a Catholic and goes to Mass every Sunday. Recently Da has been going with her, like last Sunday and the Sunday before that. It made Ma angry but he says he needs to go.

"You're not the only one going through this, Rosemary," he says to her. She throws a brush at him, but he ducks and it hits the wall. He wants to take me with him to the chapel but Ma says it isn't allowed and so I stay and eat the fairy cakes Granny's left for me; they're like little rocks but Granny likes to bake so you don't say anything, especially at the moment with everything being so strange.

Being alone with Ma isn't very nice.

"How is school?" she asks me.

"It's OK, Ma," I tell her.

She wants to ask me something else but the tears come and it makes me feel bad. I want to put my arm around her shoulder but I am afraid to touch her.

I hate that flasher. He's turned the whole world topsy-turvy, but I also think it was only a willy. Da has one and I have one. Mrs. Roy says we need them to make babies. Sometimes boys like to measure their willies, but not in front of girls because that would make them flashers too. Paul has the biggest but if it wasn't for the bend in mine I would be the biggest by far. Fat Ralph can hardly find his. Paul says it's like a pig's curly tail. Poor Ralph. Paul thinks he's so great at everything. He should try measuring it against his da's. I bet his da has a giant one and Paul's would look like a peanut next to it.

Da says Ma's a very fragile person because of the flasher. Da says we've to be very careful around her and watch what we say.

I think maybe this flasher had a really scary willy to have made her run so fast and hurt herself so badly. I hope he falls in the Clyde and drowns.

When we get to town Granny suggests Ma go to the hairdresser and get a trim. Ma has the longest hair in the world, but Granny says she has split ends and needs to get them cut. Ma agrees and off she goes to Dana's Hairsalon. Da wants to go with her but Ma says no and tells him to go for a pint.

The town is busy and it is a nice day. All the shops have their doors open and some of them have the things they want to sell in baskets outside their windows or floating from coat hangers at their doors. The pavements are swept clean and cafes have put out chairs and tables. Old ladies sit in them and have cups of tea with sticky buns. They watch everyone go by and have something to say about most of them. Granny says "Hello" to almost everyone she passes in the street.

"There are no strangers in Rothesay, Michael. Everyone knows who you are and always will. It's a blessing but it's also a curse." She says this because of the secret we are keeping about Ma's flasher.

No one is wearing a jacket on this day except Granny, who always expects rain and carries a little umbrella in her handbag. Granny decides to go to the wool shop. She makes me stand beside knitting patterns of stupid boys wearing stupid jerseys in stupid colors. She settles on a red-and-white cardigan worn by a boy she says looks like me, except he doesn't.

"It'll be perfect for the parties at Christmas," she says. I say nothing but dread wearing a knitted red jersey to the school dance where girls will say no to you when you ask them to do the Dashing White Sergeant. Also Christmas is miles away, I don't know why she's going on about it.

Later we go to Woolworths where I spend my money on pick 'n' mix. I love pick 'n' mix. Then Granny meets Mrs. Robertson and they talk for hours and I have to stand there like the invisible boy and watch all the people walk by not caring how bored to death I am. Eventually Mrs. Robertson notices me and gives me ten pence. Then she calls me a beautiful child like I'm a baby or something. I hate when she says this but it makes Granny happy, as if Mrs. Robertson said *she* was a beautiful child. Granny loves all kinds of compliments even if they're stupid ones. I remember when Ma said to her once, "Oh, I love that top, Shirley." Granny said she would lend it to her and Ma said, "Would you?" but then Da came home and Ma said, "Did you see what she was wearing, Brian?" Then they had a good laugh together and that made me glad. I like it when they laugh together even if it is about Granny and her clothes that don't suit her very well.

Granny and Mrs. Robertson talk about everything in the whole wide world. They talk about a girl who is having a baby and who doesn't have a husband. They talk about the Masonic Lodge taking up all the jobs on the island and keeping the Catholics out of work. They talk of poor souls with all kinds of troubles. And then they talk about how hard it is to be unemployed on the island and no wonder the men want a drink. And then I hear Mrs. Robertson ask Granny about Da and Ma and how they're getting on.

"Fine," Granny says. "Why wouldn't they be?"

"I heard Rosemary took a tumble, Shirley. A bad one," whispers Mrs. Robertson.

"That's right," says Granny.

Mrs. Robertson tells Granny she can tell her anything and not to forget they are good friends. She tells Granny that if she ever needs anything then she knows what door she can knock on. Granny looks annoyed and I don't understand why because Mrs. Robertson is being nice to her and has already given me ten pence.

"I don't know what you mean, Lizzy," says Granny and with a right scowl on her face.

"I just heard from Macy Kelly there had been some fighting. She said that Rosemary got hurt in the face and had to go to the hospital. Her brother Tommy told her. He took them to the hospital in his taxi apparently. She was in some state, Tommy said."

"And you think my Brian did it?"

"I'm sorry, Shirley, I shouldn't have said anything. It's just what I heard."

"My Brian wouldn't harm a hair on Rosemary's head. She fell down the stairs, and you can tell that to *Macy bloody Kelly.*"

Mrs. Robertson apologizes but Granny is furious and leaves Woolworths. I am furious and want to give the ten pence back but it is a lot of money and I decide to keep it.

"Let's go to the Tea Room," says Granny and starts walking really fast. She grabs at my hand. I hope nobody sees us but know better than to pull it away.

When we get to the Tea Room Da is already waiting for us. He smells of the sea and so I know he didn't go to the pub or he would smell of smoke and beer. It makes me feel bad for him because Da loves a pint. Granny doesn't tell him about Mrs. Robertson. She smiles at him and tells him we had a nice walk in the town. She shows him the knitting pattern and Da gives me a wink because he knows I hate it.

We wait for Ma to join us but she takes ages and so Da says I can go ahead and have my milk shake.

Eventually Ma shows up and everyone is shocked. Da looks like he's seen a ghost. I look to where Ma is peering at us through the window and I can hardly swallow my milk shake. All her lovely hair is gone. It's blond like Mrs. Connor's and cut sharp to her neck. Granny looks like she's going to fall off her chair, but Da snaps at Granny to be nice and when Ma comes into the Tea Room, Da stands up and gives her a chair like a gentleman does. At first I think Ma loves her new hair, but then she picks at it and acts like she doesn't, as if she's embarrassed she cut her hair at all. She won't even look around the Tea Room to see if there is anyone she knows or even at me sucking loud on my milk shake.

"It's lovely, Rosemary," says Granny.

"I just felt like a change," says Ma.

"Suits you well," lies Granny.

"It's beautiful, Rosemary. You look like Mia Farrow," says Da and gives her a kiss on the cheek. "Let's have a nice cup of tea."

This cheers Ma up but Granny keeps looking at the other tea drinkers and so do I. When Mary Frankel in her flowery pink apron comes to take our order, she gives Ma a big smile and tells her she looks fantastic, but she also makes a tiny little face at the scars on Ma's lip and face. She tells Ma to turn round so she can see the back of her head. She tells Ma she never looked better.

"Now what can I get you?" says Mary and gives Da a look

31

so bad he goes as red as a raspberry. Granny acts like she doesn't notice a thing but she does.

I have fish and chips. My favorite. Ma has a scone and doesn't eat it. Da tries Mary's lasagna to be friendly and Granny has some toast and a cup of tea. It's nearly the best day I've had in ages and I look forward to eating my pick 'n' mix as soon as I get home, but Ma wants to go for a walk along the shore and that's what we do. We walk as far as Craigmore and I feel as if my legs will fall off. The sea air tastes salty and it's a wee bit chilly. Granny has to sit down a few times because she's so tired. Da has enough of it in the end, although Ma looks like she could walk for miles.

Da decides we will get a taxi on the way back and I am so excited. We will roll into the car park of Barone in a huge black cab. Everyone will be so jealous that we can afford one. I can hardly wait to see the look on Paul MacDonald's face. He'll be mad and crazy with envy. His family can hardly afford the electricity meter in their house and I have pick 'n' mix in my pocket. I will have friends again because everyone likes pick 'n' mix and I still have ten pence left for the ice cream van. Marianne will let me back into the talent show if I share my sweets and Ma will start talking and smiling again. I feel happier than I have felt in ages. I love Woolworths, but I hate Mrs. Robertson and I hate Mary Frankel for the look she gave my da. I also hate my ma's new hair and wish it was long again. I feel bad about that.

seven

Paul MacDonald wants to fight me in the Woody near our houses for telling on him and Marianne for being disgusting behind the shed. We call it the Woody even though it looks more like a swamp than a wood, but it does have a tree. It also has bramble bushes and raspberry bushes but you're not allowed to eat from them because of the worms inside. I hate the bushes anyway; they scratch at your legs and you can't avoid them because you have to go cut through them to get to the Woody.

There is lots of long grass in the Woody, as tall as a man, and girls won't play there because of the snakes. I've never seen a snake but we tell the girls there are plenty of them and that we've seen a ton. We also tell them there are rats. I've not seen a rat either but I have seen a couple of mice and they're really cute but a girl would go mad if she saw one. All this stuff is important because it keeps girls away when we're playing soldiers or haunted wood. Grown-ups use the Woody as a dump, but not like for nasty rubbish you have in your bin like eggshells and potato peelings, but for things they don't want in their houses anymore, like freezers and tables.

Dirty Alice doesn't care about snakes and long grass, she's always playing in the Woody. If her ma was alive she'd give her a hiding but she's dead now and her da doesn't care where she goes. Her brother Luke cares and he's always yelling at her to do this thing or that thing but Dirty Alice doesn't listen and Luke gets fed up chasing her around. Luke has no friends but it's his own fault for being so clever.

"He's the cleverest boy in the town," says Da. "He plays chess. Why don't you play chess, Michael? Maybe Alice's brother could teach you."

"I don't like chess," I tell him and I don't. Mrs. Roy already tried to teach me in class and only the suck-ups could do it, so Luke must be a suck-up.

"You could try," says Da.

"Leave the boy alone. If he doesn't want to play chess he doesn't have to play chess," says Ma.

"I'm only saying," says Da, who shuffles at his paper and complains about the war.

"Maybe Michael can learn cards," says Granny.

"I don't want to play cards. I want to play soccer."

"Then away out and play soccer," says Ma.

Ma is always chasing me out of the house. She's always chasing Da. Sometimes she gives him money for the pub but he always gives it back. He's started going for walks to the loch. I go with him and we talk about his childhood and all the things he loved to do as a boy. He shows me a tree where there used to be a swing, but it's gone now. He tells me he broke his arm on the tree and made Granny cry. He tells me about a teacher who lived in a house we pass while going to the loch, a teacher who smacked his arse with a belt. He is glad teachers can't do that anymore. He says it is a good law that strangers, even a teacher, can't touch another man's child and then he tells me how sore it is to get the strap on your hands. Da tells me about Grandpa Jake, who had five brothers and two sisters and no money and who had soup for his dinner all the time. Da tells me about his grandpa, my great-grandpa, who went to war and never came back, leaving my great-grandma Eliza to fend for herself. Da says she died when she was a very old woman because she was tough as nails.

When we get to the loch Da says we'll go fishing sometime, but I know we won't. It's just what he says. It's always muddy at the loch and when we get home it's dinnertime and we have to leave our shoes at the door. Granny says it's good to go to the loch because it will make you have a good sleep at night, but sometimes it is hard to sleep because Ma screams so much, not all the time, but sometimes. Da can calm her down with nice words and a cup of tea, but if he can't he has to sleep on the sofa. She says no one understands and Da says she should have gone to the police. This makes her go crazy and she wakes the whole house from their beds. Granny will come into my room to tell me everything is OK. Eventually Ma goes back to sleep but Da still has to sleep on the sofa. It's not fair. He wasn't the one who flashed her.

When Paul MacDonald meets me in the Woody he brings a lot of people who hate me, except Fat Ralph, who is on my side. He hates Paul MacDonald worse than me. The girls come because they like to see boys fighting. Marianne is there and acting like it's all over her and it is, I suppose, but I hate that she's standing next to Paul and is all dramatic, as if she can't stand it when she's really loving the whole thing. Tracey and

Fiona hold on to her so she doesn't faint. Dirty Alice is grinning her head off and telling Paul to give me a good thumping. I hate Dirty Alice and I wish I was fighting her.

No one knows how to start the fight and so I take a run at Paul. He falls on his arse. I jump on top of him and slap his face. He grabs at my hair and punches the air. We roll about and it's all slapping and hard hitting but no one is winning. Then Paul cuts his lip on something and there's blood. I must have scratched him. He stops fighting then and starts to scream.

"Look what you did to my lip." Everyone is shocked and then Dirty Alice says, "He's just like his da."

I tell Dirty Alice to shut up and then she says, "Everyone knows he gave your ma a right doing. It's in the family, battering folk. I suppose you want to batter me. Go ahead. I dare you." She shoves her face in my face and points at her chin, but I walk away and I'm nearly crying but I can't cry because the first one to cry is the loser of the fight and I am not the loser because Paul is bleeding. I want to yell out my da never hit my ma. I want to tell them about the flasher and the terrible fall, but I am not allowed. My da would give me a hiding and my ma would start screaming.

"I gave you a doing," I say to Paul.

"No, I gave you a doing," Paul says.

"Who's bleeding?" I say. "Not me."

"Let's start again," says Dirty Alice.

I don't want to. I'm too tired, but I still act like I do. So I look hard and say OK. Paul goes red and shakes his head.

"I'm going home," he says and starts to cry like a baby. Then he walks away limping, even though it's his lip that got cut. Fat Ralph shouts out, "Michael is the winner." Marianne looks back at me to let me know she isn't pleased about it and runs after Paul to hold him up. Fiona and Tracey help her. Paul's acting all wounded like a soldier I machine-gunned in the Woody when we were playing Falklands that time. He's a big faker and I want to shout it out loud but there's been enough fighting and I want to go home.

"Everyone still hates you," snips Dirty Alice.

"Away and have a bath, you stinky cow," I say.

Alice is all red and gives me the finger. "Fuck off," she spits.

"No, you fuck off," I say.

Then Katie Calderwood dumping a TV in the Woody goes mad and tells us we can't say "fuck" to each other or she'll tell our mas and our das, except Dirty Alice doesn't have a ma and her da never opens the door, so it's all right for her.

I go home straightaway but Paul MacDonald's ma has already been on the phone and told my ma about the fight, but Ma tells Paul MacDonald's ma a few things about her "precious son" and doesn't care too much I thumped him. Later she tells me it's good I stood up for myself and that Paul Mac-Donald needed a good hiding. I am still worried Katie Calderwood will tell on me for saying "fuck" to Dirty Alice, but Katie Calderwood doesn't say a word. She just walks past our window and gives me a bad look. I feel worried for saying "fuck" and also scared because one day when I'm least expecting it Katie Calderwood might tell Ma and Da, maybe when it's my birthday and then I wouldn't get anything. If she did that, I would hate her forever and I'd tell her she looks like a man. She would hate that because she thinks she looks like a woman. I wish I'd never said "fuck" to anyone in my life.

eight

When you fight the toughest kid in the land and win, then you are the toughest kid in the land, except girls don't care about that. Marianne wants me to say sorry to Paul. She says if I say sorry then I can be in the talent show, although that's never going to happen, but just in case it does I go look for Paul. I find him playing with Fat Ralph in the Woody, but I don't say sorry to him, I just ask to play soldiers. Paul says yes straightaway. He doesn't want to fight again either, so we decide to shoot Fat Ralph, but Ralph hates being machine-gunned to the ground all the time and says he doesn't want to play anymore and we decide to go find the girls. Marianne is in tears because Bardo lost the Eurovision Song Contest and someone called Nicole from Germany won with a song about peace instead. Dirty Alice isn't crying. She's screaming it was a fix because of the war we're having in the Falklands. She's acting like she knows stuff about wars and Margaret Thatcher just like my da does, but she doesn't, my da is the only person in the whole town who knows these things. He is a political person and says so. Dirty Alice doesn't know anything. Everything she says gets on my nerves, even her face. It's all screwed up and sweaty, as if she was running somewhere. She's stupid, that Dirty Alice, and she's always falling over on her arse. "It's because of those long skinny legs," Ma says. If I hear a loud crying I don't even have to look up, I know it's Dirty Alice all hunched up like a ball sucking at her knee. Mrs. Connor helped her one time and took her to her house for a plaster, but Ma said that was wrong and we should never go to anyone's house by ourselves.

"Everyone knows Mrs. Connor, Ma," I say.

"But what if she has a stranger with her, then what? She's always running around with this one and that one."

"What do you mean, Ma?"

Granny and Ma give each other a look, a look that means something I can't know. They never tell me anything. Everything I find out is by accident and it's not fair because I can keep a secret better than anyone.

"Away out with your ball, Michael," says Granny.

Anyway, Tracey and her mad red hair tells Marianne Bardo's song was the best by far and we should sing it in the talent show. This cheers Marianne up and then I tell her it doesn't matter anyway because there will be other times we'll win the Eurovision Contest because Britain is brilliant at everything.

"Bucks Fizz won, didn't they? And we had a great song to sing for a really long time," I say.

Everyone agrees and Marianne sniffs a yes. Dirty Alice feels left out and moves in to comfort Marianne but is pushed off by Lanky Fiona. I'm glad about that, Dirty Alice is always hogging Marianne like she owns her or something.

Next thing Tracey is singing "Making Your Mind Up" and at first Marianne pretends she doesn't want to because she's so upset about Bardo but it's obvious she's dying to get up there with Fiona and Tracey and so she wipes her face and starts dancing, even Dirty Alice is in there, and you should have seen them waving their skirts about and doing what girls do with songs. They don't care, girls, even when there's no music, it's just them singing and jumping about. They move in circles and wrap themselves around one another. They spin about and lift their skirts until we nearly see their knickers. I see Dirty Alice's knickers. They're white. I hate her knickers. Then they grab at each other's hands and run about all over the place doing high kicks and all kinds of things. I like Adam and the Ants. Adam is like a soldier, although my da isn't keen on the glossy lips he has. My ma thinks Adam's beautiful and Granny doesn't care for him at all. I think Adam Ant is amazing and when I'm alone in my room I put on the record Da got for me and I jump up and down and pretend I have a guitar. I kick my legs and fling my arms over my head like Adam does and I think I'm the best singer in the world. It's good to listen to your records when no one is looking.

Watching the girls dancing is all right but we still act like we think they're eejits and make faces at them. Paul actually falls over making sick noises, but then he laughs to show he was just kidding around, the girls love that. He's such a suck-up, that Paul, and he still likes Marianne even though I've thumped him for it. I would never have sucked up like that. I would have kept the vomit noise real and made the girls feel like they were stupid. You can't be too mad for girls. I mean it's OK to show up places you think they'll be but you don't go to their doors and ask if they want to come out for a while. The talent show is different because I'm doing keepy-uppies and we're all getting some money from it. It's five pence a ticket.

My granny says this is a scandalous amount of money and will only pay one pence.

When I get home Da is all angry like Dirty Alice was and saying the Eurovision Song Contest was fixed because of the war and it was Margaret Thatcher's fault we lost and if Ma wants to blame anyone, then it should be the prime minister.

"They were wonderful dancers," cries Ma.

"And very good-looking," says Granny.

Da says Ma's silly for crying and it's only a song. Also he liked the German girl and her little guitar, but not as much as Jan Leeming, who reads the news and was at the Eurovision Song Contest in a beautiful dress telling everyone about the points each country was winning.

"She's a fine woman, all right," says Da.

Ma pulls a face at him, but that's how it is with Ma right now. She makes faces and leaves rooms all the time, usually for a bath or a nap.

"If she just went to the police," whispers Da. "If she just told the truth she'd feel better."

"You mean you would," says Granny.

"We all would," says Da.

"You should have told the police from the start, didn't I tell you to? Then all the neighbors wouldn't be thinking you smack your wife around. It's too late to go back now."

"Why is that?" quizzes Da.

"No one would believe her is why. It's been left too long. They might think she made it up or she's mad or some-thing. They might think we're all mad. We should have said something as soon as she walked through that door, but we didn't. It's done, Brian. Leave it be. They'll be no more talking about this family. I won't have it."

Da looks angry.

"This too shall pass," says Granny and crosses herself.

"When will it pass? When?"

I think the same as Da. When will this all go away? Ma's not being nice to any of us.

"Give the girl time for Christ's sake. It's been less than two months. Be patient."

Da looks sorry when Granny says that and hides in his paper. I don't feel sorry at all, two months was a long time ago, it was dark then and the sun is shining now. Da walks everywhere with her. She's safe now. We won't let anyone hurt her, not ever again.

nine

Ma knits like Granny and hardly looks at anyone. Da tries to act like normal. Ma says she's knitting for Christmas, but it's only May and Christmas is way off, they'll have us knitted to death by then. I hate getting jerseys and itchy socks anyway. I especially hate mittens. They always get wet in the snow and never keep your fingers warm. I hope no one knits me mittens.

Da says a scarf will be handy and hopes Ma is knitting one for him.

"It's cold for spring," he says.

"It's practically the summer," says Ma.

"Ne'er cast a clout till May is out," says Granny.

Everyone agrees it's still a bit cold, except me, I'm always hot from running around with my soccer ball. I love soccer and I'm going to play for Celtic one day. Da agrees.

"You're as good as Paul McStay any day of the week, just keep practicing the dribbling."

Da walks Ma to work and back again every night since the flasher. I think this is a nice thing to do but Ma doesn't. She calls Da possessive. Granny says this means you're loved a lot and I wonder why Ma doesn't like it.

Ma is also doing the Open University thing they do on the

telly. She's learning all about books and stuff. This annoys Da. Granny says it is good to keep yourself busy.

Ma says she is reading Shakespeare. Mrs. Roy says Shakespeare had a beard and was a wonderful playwright. He sounds boring to me. Ma is boring. I want to know if she'll come to the talent show but she just says, "Maybe."

"And where else will you be, Rosemary?" snips Da.

"It's a long time to be practicing, Michael," says Ma. "Months and months now."

"It's maybe nearly soon," I say, even though I know it isn't anywhere near soon and might never happen at all, but she doesn't say anything, not to any of us, it's like we didn't speak.

Da says he can't wait, neither can Granny.

"Marianne's taking her time with the talent show, Ma, she wants it to be perfect," I say, but the truth is I think the same as Ma. I don't think the talent show will ever happen, like it's something the girls are just playing at to get attention.

Ma doesn't care about the talent show anyway, she just knits and reads and has her baths, except one Saturday night when Tricia Law comes to the house holding a cigarette, causing an uproar.

"Is Rosemary ready?" she says.

"For what?" says Da.

Then Ma appears smelling really nice and says, "I'm off out for a drink with Tricia. I told you this afternoon," she says.

"You told me no such thing," says Da.

"What's the matter, Brian? Can your wife not pop down the road for a quick one?"

"Without her husband?" he says.

"That's right," says Tricia. "Without her husband."

Tricia looks annoyed at Da and Granny is looking like she wants to push Tricia through the front door.

"Then get a taxi home," he whispers to Ma.

"I'll walk her," says Tricia.

"And who'll walk you, Tricia?" says Da.

"I'm a big girl," says Tricia.

"A taxi for the pair of you. There and back. I'll pay for it."

"Isn't he the gent?" laughs Tricia.

Tricia has already been drinking beer, I can tell because she is swinging a bit on her hips like Granny does when she drinks lager at New Year's.

When Tricia and Ma go away to the pub, Granny puts her hand on Da's shoulder and tells him Ma will come round and be back to normal in no time, but Da is annoyed and grabs for his coat.

"Where are you going?" says Granny.

"For a drink," says Da.

"Don't do that, Brian. She'll go mad if she thinks you're following her. This is a good thing, son. She's getting on with her life. It's what she needs."

"Since when did my Rosemary ever go to bars without her husband? These are all new things she's doing! The haircut. The Shakespeare. The knitting till her hands hurt. It's not getting on with life, Ma. She's erasing who she was. She's pretending what happened to her happened to someone else and not the woman with the blond cropped hair."

They are talking about the flasher again and when they remember I am standing there in my pajamas they stop. Da strokes my head and suggests we have some hot chocolate.

Granny makes terrible hot chocolate. It's all watery, just

like her stew, but Da doesn't mind because she slips whiskey into his. We have some fairy cakes and Da asks about the talent show again. He asks me to show him some keepy-uppies, but I bounce the ball into the sink and annoy Granny. Da thinks it's funny. I tell him all about Marianne and all the things she's going to be doing in the show and about how upset she is about Bardo losing the Eurovision Song Contest just like Ma was. Everyone looks sorry for Marianne and for Ma.

"The Eurovision Song Contest has upset a lot of people, son. A lot of people," says Da. "Now off to bed."

I do as I'm told, but I want to stay up for hours and hours with them. I like to talk to Granny and Da, but before I'm even off my chair the doorbell rings.

"Can I get the door, Da? Can I?" I beg.

I love to answer the door, but when I open it I find Ma with Tricia and Kenny Stuart's da, who drives the ambulance about the town. Kenny thinks this is a brilliant job, as if his da is a doctor or something, but he's really just a taxi driver for the hospital.

"Jesus, what happened, Rosemary? You're as white as a sheet, lassie," says Granny, grabbing at Ma.

"She collapsed in the Bull," says Tricia.

"Drunk?" yells Da at Ma.

"She never touched a drop," snaps Tricia.

Ma looks scared.

"She fainted, must have been the heat in the place. She's OK now. We took her up to the hospital and had her checked out," says Kenny's da.

"And you couldn't have called the house?" says Da.

Ma starts to babble and everyone is staring at her.

"I couldn't stand it, Shirley. All those people, so many of them," she cries.

"I think she must be coming down with some sort of virus," whispers Kenny's da. "Best put her to bed, Brian."

"What's wrong with me?" Ma asks Da.

"It's OK, love," Da says and takes Ma upstairs.

"What's going on round here?" says Tricia. "That lassie hasn't been the same since your precious Brian gave her a hiding."

"I'm away, Shirley," Kenny's da says. He doesn't want to hear Tricia talking like that to Granny and neither do I.

"Hope Rosemary gets better soon," he says to Granny.

Kenny's da is out of sight in no time, but Tricia won't leave.

"My Brian never laid a finger on her. She fell down the very steps you're standing on."

Granny reddens and it looks like she's telling a fib and she is but not like Tricia thinks.

"She's my friend, Shirley, you remember that, and I won't have anyone hurting her again, right?"

"My Brian wouldn't let the wind blow on Rosemary. Now get the hell off my doorstep!"

Tricia goes all red and leaves, but you can tell she wants to say something else but can't think of anything. Tricia swaggers away; she's had a few for sure. Granny shakes her head at her, like when Da says something he shouldn't to Ma or when I won't eat my dinner or when Ma uses up all the hot water.

"How you getting home, Tricia?" Granny shouts after her.

"What the fuck do you care?"

"I don't care, but that's some state to be walking around in by yourself. Anything could happen."

Granny's thinking of the flasher and so am I.

"Then phone us a taxi," slurs Tricia.

"Fine," says Granny and dials for a car.

Tricia sits on the pavement next to the lamppost outside our house. She looks orange. She lights herself a cigarette and she's staring at me through the open door; that's when Granny closes it so I can't see her anymore, but I can still smell Tricia's smoke.

"Would you go to bed?!" screams Granny.

In Ma and Da's room I can hear Ma sobbing her heart out.

"I couldn't swallow and I couldn't breathe. Everyone was looking at me. At this face, Brian. At these scars."

"It's all right, Rosemary. You're home now. You're home."

It goes on like this for a long time, Ma saying stuff and Da telling her it's all right until I'm almost asleep, but then Da comes into my room. He sits at the bottom of my bed and puts his head in his hands.

"Are you all right, Da?" I say.

"Away and sleep, son," he says.

"Is Ma asleep?" I ask.

He nods and I think he might cry or something and I really don't want him to, not in front of me. I couldn't stand it.

"Hey, Da," I say, "I saw Tricia Law going into the bushes with Skinny Rab!"

Da gives me the funniest look.

"I did," I say. "I swear it."

I tell him the whole story and he laughs. He laughs harder than I've heard him laugh in a long time.

"Skinny Rab and Tricia Law?" His eyes are wet with laughing and I feel like the funniest boy on Caledonia Walk.

"Michael," he says and I know he's going to tell me something important, "don't be telling anyone else that story, mind, that's our little secret. You're a man now. Only women tell tales like that and usually to other women. Men know how to keep their lips buttoned and you have to keep your lips buttoned all the time. You understand?"

I know he's talking about the flasher again and I nod. It seems everything is about the flasher.

"Da," I say, "is Ma going to be OK?"

He starts to say something else, but before he can answer, Ma starts yelling. He runs away then and forgets to turn the light off, but I leave it on because I don't want to sleep in the dark, not with Ma screaming in the other room.

ten

D a brings home a puppy called Frankie. Ma loves him. I love him. Granny hates the sight of him but since it makes Ma happy she gives her best smile and feeds him the leftover stew. The dog loves her stew. This makes Granny like him a little bit more.

The dog is Ma's protector and my best pal. He is a black Lab and everyone wants to pet him. Da says he paid a pretty penny for him. Ma likes that Da spent money on the dog because Da never spends money on anything and Da loves how pleased Ma is to have her own dog. During the day Ma and I try to teach him tricks and at night when Ma goes to work, she and Da take the dog with them up the high street. Frankie makes people stop on the road and talk to Ma and Da like normal, it's like people like you better with a cute dog and they forget things.

"He's not big now, Michael, but he'll get big," says Ma.

"How big?" I say.

"As big as this!" and she opens her arms and grabs at me. I get shy in my mother's arms, especially when she holds me so tight I feel I might suffocate. She lets me go and gives me a wink. It's the nicest she's been in ages.

Frankie sleeps in Ma and Da's bed, but it's mostly Ma's bed.

Da sleeps downstairs. I wish Frankie slept with me. Sometimes he jumps on my covers and you can see him thinking about having a wee nap but then he hears Ma coming up the stairs and away he goes to be with her. Ma and Da are friendlier to each other because of Frankie and he's made everything a bit great again. Granny is mad because he's not toilet-trained and leaves a mess for her to clean up but I've seen Da clean tons of it. We mostly open the back door and let him go in the yard. Da says it's good for the flowers except we hardly have any flowers. Da keeps promising to get to it but he never does.

"It's not like you don't have the time," says Ma.

This makes my tummy go funny when she says this because she's said something mean to Da and when everything seemed a bit brilliant again.

"I'll get round to it, Rosemary," Da promises.

Ma pats the dog and says she wants to take him for a walk by herself along the shore. This makes Da a wee bit hurt but he agrees and Ma takes Frankie down to the beach.

While Ma's with Frankie Da goes down to the hardware store and buys a shovel and some fertilizer, some seeds for nice flowers and starts to dig the whole garden up, but then it starts to rain and the whole garden turns into a swamp and when Ma gets back it makes her laugh and she pats Da on the back for trying. I've never seen him so pleased, but then Tricia Law comes to the house and he is less pleased. She comes to apologize to Granny for her bad behavior. She brings flowers and looks really sore for being so nasty and drunk. Ma hugs her and invites her in because they're still best friends. Granny and Tricia light their fags and Ma makes everyone a cup of tea, but I still hate her. I don't care if she's Ma's friend, she goes in the bushes with Marianne's da and she's not nice to mine. It's a good day for Ma though, she loves to talk, but Da is nervous around Tricia and her "big gob" and hides in the living room watching soccer. I join him and Da gives me a look and we have a wee laugh together about Tricia and Skinny Rab, but then Da pulls himself together and chases me while he does his betting coupon. It's Da's dream to win the pools one day and go to Disneyland. It's also my dream. Ma says he could take us tomorrow if he wanted but Da reminds her his old man's money is for something special. This makes Ma sulk because the only special thing she can think of is having her own house.

I stand at the door and listen to Tricia Law gossip about all kinds of things but mostly about Dirty Alice's da, who has opened his curtains and is going to the pub. This makes everyone pleased for him.

"He's getting out and about. Best thing for him," says Ma.

"But he gets very drunk," says Tricia.

"Is that a fact?" says Granny in a funny voice.

"No need for sarcasm, Shirley. Haven't I said I'm sorry already?" says Tricia.

"Ah, come on, Shirley. She didn't know what she was saying," says Ma.

"Go on with the story," nips Granny.

"Anyway, last Saturday he was seen with that Connor woman, arm in arm staggering up the road after a wild night in the Ascog Disco. She did everything except pull her knickers off and stick them to the ceiling."

"Disgusting," says Granny.

I have not peeked through Mrs. Connor's window in a long time and I feel bad about her throwing her knickers about.

On a day like this, drinking tea with Tricia and laughing about Mrs. Connor, Ma seems to be getting better, but when Tricia leaves, Ma will grab for her books again or her knitting. She's also stopped smoking. I'm glad. I hate cigarettes. I especially hate being sent to the shops for them all the time. It's boring and there's never any change left over for some sweets.

Granny says, "It's because the flasher smoked. She can't abide the smell anymore. A shame, that, because she always liked a good smoke."

I don't think it has anything to do with the flasher because everyone Ma knows smokes, including Granny. I agree with Da and think it is because Ma wants to be someone else since she was flashed at, as if being someone else will make it go away. I wish I could make the flasher go away, he has caused no end of trouble for us all.

Da is pleased Ma has stopped smoking because she smoked more than anyone and he was getting sick of all the yellow on the ceilings and on the white porcelain Wally dogs Ma got from her own ma and da when they were alive, when she wasn't an orphan.

Ma also prefers to drink coffee, which I love because it smells so nice. She says it keeps her awake. Da says she shouldn't drink it at night but that's when Ma drinks it the most. She says it helps her with her studies. She says she doesn't get a minute to herself to read during the day and of course she works at the school in the evening.

Ma has a professor and everything. She talks about him all the time. It makes Da annoyed.

"Well, isn't that dandy?" he'll say when she tells a professor story. Ma just ignores him.

Ma likes to keep herself busy. Granny says it's good to be busy and that it takes the mind off sad things.

"Like Grandpa Jake?" I ask Granny.

"That's right, like Grandpa Jake, but sometimes it's hard, son, the mind can be cruel and you can't help thinking about lost things."

"What kind of lost things?"

"Don't you ask a lot of questions, Michael Murray?"

I don't expect her to say anything more but then she says to me, "I miss dancing with him. He was a good dancer, your grandpa."

I feel sad when she says that because whenever she is stirring at the watery stew she sways like a boat to the radio. She is dreaming of dancing with Grandpa Jake. This is why Granny takes such a long time to make the stew I think: chopping the carrots and peeling the onions, frying the meat and adding the flour. It can take forever sometimes. I still wish it would take a hundred years because I hate to eat it, even if it does bring her closer to Grandpa Jake. I bet he hated it too.

eleven

Mrs. Roy says I am too quiet for my own good and makes Da come to school. Ma is busy with her studies and can't come.

"I'm sorry, Michael. I've a ton of work to do. Da can go," says Ma.

"Can I?" says Da.

Ma almost growls at him but settles on a dirty look instead.

I don't want anyone to go, but I still think mas should see teachers and not das. Da thinks the same and is angry at Mrs. Roy for dragging him all the way to our school from Barone because it's a long walk and he will have to do it all over again in the evening when he walks Ma to work with Frankie.

Sitting with Mrs. Roy and Da feels strange to me. Da can hardly sit on the seat she gives him because it's only for boys and girls and not my da with his huge arse and fat legs. I sit next to Da but Mrs. Roy suggests I play a game or something because she wants to talk about me.

"It's the noisy kids you need to watch out for," says Da.

Mrs. Roy says, "It is the quiet children who need the most attention."

Mrs. Roy tells Da I used to be very noisy but now I am as quiet as a lamb. She says she is worried about my schoolwork and I never finish anything I start. She wants to send work home. I don't want her to send work home. I can't play soccer then. I hope Da says no. He doesn't and it makes me not want to talk to him ever again.

"A lamb she called him," says Da to Granny.

Granny laughs and Ma smirks. This makes me mad at Ma because she wasn't even there.

"Is that right?" Ma says to me. "Wish you were a lamb around here." She gives me a wink and I ignore her. She doesn't even notice. She just writes her little words in her little notepad because she is studying and not caring about anything except her schoolwork and her stupid professor.

"Cheeky cow asked if there was anything going on at home," says Da. "I told her to mind her business, but I knew what she was getting at."

Granny nods in my direction and reminds Da I am sitting there having a scone, even though I know what they are talking about and how everyone thinks Da beat my ma, even Mrs. Roy.

The next day at school I am noisy. I jump on my school chair and sing Celtic songs. Then I call Mrs. Roy the worst name I can think of. The headmistress is called and Da has to collect me from school. I am suspended for a week.

It is one of the greatest shames to be suspended. It's like saying I will go to jail and I am a terrible boy who will become a criminal one day. Ma gets very upset and Granny says she doesn't know what she's going to do with me. They are worried about the neighbors and what people in the town will say.

"Like they're not saying enough about us already," cries Granny.

Da says nothing at all and takes me to the loch with Frankie.

It is a quiet walk. He doesn't say anything about standing on a chair or singing Celtic songs at the top of my voice and he especially doesn't say anything about me calling Mrs. Roy "a fucking old witch with bushy hair."

"It's going to be OK," he tells me.

I know he is talking about Ma and himself and the town and all the other things it is wrong to mention. I want to cry, but I also want to be brave for my da. I tell him I am sorry for being bad and I will be a better boy. He gives me a hug and tells me to do my best.

Even though it starts to rain, we go all the way round the loch, but it's a warm rain and I don't mind one bit, but then Da wants to go through the park where Ma was flashed.

"No, Da," I say, "let's go down the high street and get some chips."

He doesn't want to, he wants to walk through the park and find the flasher, and so he steps on the grass with Frankie, but Frankie sinks into a puddle of mud and gets so dirty Da has to pull him away with the lead. He looks into the park and shakes his head.

"Let's go get something to eat," he says.

We walk away and I am glad.

twelve

I can't see Mrs. Connor dance. Dirty Alice threw a stone through Mrs. Connor's bedroom window and tried to blame me. Luckily Fat Ralph saw the whole thing and everyone was very sorry to me. I got twenty pence from Ma and Da and a chocolate biscuit from Mrs. Connor, who had really yelled at me and nearly made me cry. My ma was very angry at Mrs. Connor afterward and I was pleased.

"I think I should go over there and say something to her. Cheeky cow."

"You thought it too," says Da.

"So did you," says Ma back at him.

"I never thought it," says Granny, which was true. Granny grabbed on to me while they were all shouting and told them all to leave me alone.

Now the window's all boarded up.

Da says Dirty Alice is all crazy because her dad is over there all the time digging and fixing things for Mrs. Connor, like the window Dirty Alice smashed. Mrs. Connor brings Mr. McFadden tea and biscuits while he holds a big shovel or is standing on a ladder for her. Da says it is good Dirty Alice's da is getting on with his life, but Granny and Ma think it's disgusting because they don't like Mrs. Connor, even though they smile and wave at her every time she walks by the house.

"Maria would turn in her grave," says Granny.

"Maria would be glad her husband has a bit of company," says Da.

"There's a lot of men on this island who've had *her* company," says Ma.

Ma has made a joke and it's a big thing in the house because she barely laughs at anything anymore. This makes Granny laugh harder to remind Ma how funny she can be. I don't think it is funny; it's a mean thing to say about Mrs. Connor. Da thinks the same and I am so mad I go play with my soccer ball.

Mr. McFadden likes Mrs. Connor a lot because I've seen him smiling at her when she's walking away from him. I saw my da smiling at my ma when she was walking away from him once, but I don't think she liked it.

"What do you think you're looking at?" said Ma.

"Nothing at all," said Da.

Luke wasn't there when his da was staring at Mrs. Connor but I don't think he would have gone mad or anything like Dirty Alice did. Luke likes it at Mrs. Connor's house. He has his tea there sometimes; so does Dirty Alice but she sits in the yard with a plate on her lap. Mrs. Connor must hate her and love Luke because he's so clever. Luke really sucks up to grown-ups. They love him and always say nice things about him.

"Takes flowers to his mother's grave every Sunday since she passed," says Granny.

"A beautiful boy," says Ma.

Ma cries whenever she sees Luke walk by with his flowers. Granny crosses herself. Da says, "A fine lad." I play keepy-uppies and don't look, especially when he's dragging Dirty Alice with him.

Mrs. Connor will probably marry Mr. McFadden now and have babies. Dirty Alice won't like that one bit and neither will I. Mr. McFadden will catch me if I look through the window and I'll get my arse tanned, but worse than that, everyone will know I'm peeping at Mrs. Connor.

thirteen

Ma goes to college in Greenock. Da hates it. She takes her books in the leather bag that used to belong to Grandpa Jake. She goes early in the morning on the six-thirty boat and comes back at five in the evening in time for tea. Then she's off to work to clean the school floors. At night she is exhausted and falls straight to sleep.

"You'll kill yourself at this rate," says Granny to Ma.

"It's worth it. I'm learning so much, Shirley."

"Like what?" says Granny.

"Shakespeare. You should see how badly women get treated in his plays. S'terrible."

"What do you mean?"

"Well, they're not free, are they? They're always passed from father to husband. And they're never trusted, sometimes they're murdered."

"Murdered, you say? Jesus save us."

"Sounds like a load of shite to me," says Da.

Ma ignores him and I ignore Ma. She's never around these days and always off somewhere. Da says she's running away from herself but then he gets a look from Granny, which means he shouldn't say things like that around me, like the scandal of Tricia and Skinny Rab. When it all came out, Da and I just tittered and winked at each other. We were secretly glad Tricia and Skinny Rab had gotten themselves caught for running into bushes together. We don't like Tricia anymore, even if Ma does.

Now everyone knows about it, especially all the kids. It's all out and whispered about behind dirty wee hands.

Kids are mostly not allowed to know anything about grown-up stuff. Marianne's ma and da are probably fighting about it every night but Marianne will be asleep or pretending it's just a normal fight. She'll ignore the stuff about Tricia Law and she'll be glad when her da says sorry to her ma. She'll pretend and hope everything is fixed so she can get on with the talent show that's never going to happen anyway. She will never cry, not in front of us, and she will never tell, even though we all know anyway because most of us listen at doors. Sometimes I imagine Luke and Dirty Alice finding out about their ma having cancer while listening at a door or maybe they were sat down and told properly. Probably not. Kids are always the last to know anything, except me. "He's quiet on his feet all right," says Ma and looks at me suspiciously.

When they want to speak really privately, they sometimes stop midsentence and Granny will say, "Little jugs have big lugs." I'm sent from the room with the door firmly closed then, but I listen anyway, my ear pushed against the wood paneling.

Granny says Marianne's ma might leave the island now.

"She only came here for him, you know?" says Granny.

"I think she'll stay," says Ma. "For the child," she whispers.

"Well, I think she should leave for the child. A woman never forgets a thing like that, and all they'll do is fight in front of her and mess her little head up. I say move on and be done with it," says Da.

"What do you know about moving on?" snaps Ma.

"More than you do," cracks Da.

"Fuck you, Brian," snaps Ma.

Da doesn't shuffle his paper this time. He slaps it on the table and off he storms from the kitchen again. He almost catches me at the door but I get away in time. He'd go mad if he caught me spying.

After my dinner I go to the car park to practice my keepy-uppies and find Dirty Alice drawing with a stick on the gravel. I sneak up behind her and find her drawing a love heart. I want to run and not see, but she'd hear me, so I scare her out of her wits and give her time to rub out the heart in the gravel.

She screams at me. "What did you do that for?"

"I want to practice my keepy-uppies and you're in my way. Where is everyone anyway?"

"In for their tea," says Dirty Alice.

"Why are you not in for your tea?" I ask.

"Because Louisa Connor is in there making us shite and peas to eat and I won't touch her food. I won't."

"That's daft," I say. "You'll starve."

"I hate her."

"You can still hate her and have your dinner," I say.

Dirty Alice thinks on this while her tummy grumbles like mad. "You think you're so clever, don't you?"

"I'm cleverer than you," I say. "Why did you blame me for the broken window, Alice? Did you really think people would believe I'd do something like that? It was stupid of you."

She goes red. "I'm sorry, Michael," she says. "I didn't mean it. I was just mad at stupid Louisa Connor."

"She's a nice lady. You'll get used to her." My ball slips from my knee and rolls under a car.

"You're rubbish at keepy-uppies," Alice snips and then walks away to her house so she can chew on her shite and peas and still hate Louisa Connor. She's a bitch, that Alice, even if she is sorry for blaming me for crimes I did not commit.

I think Louisa is the most beautiful name in the world and when I have a baby one day I hope it will be a girl with hair like Blondie's and a face like Mrs. Connor's.

I practice my keepy-uppies like mad and Marianne, who has finished her tea, comes out to the car park. I think she's going to practice her songs, but she doesn't, she watches me do my keepy-uppies for a while and I love it. She looks like she's never seen such skill.

"I'm going to play for Celtic one day," I tell her.

"I bet you do, Michael," she says.

I love that she says this.

"Do you like me, Michael?" she says.

I almost faint.

"You're all right," I say but my heart is thumping like a ball on concrete.

"You want to go somewhere with me?" she says.

"Where?" I say.

"Down there," she says.

It's the bushes, the long bushes where no one can see you. It's where kissing and all sorts of things go on and if someone sees you coming out of the bushes with a girl you get the hiding of your life and the girl is kept indoors forever and ever.

It's worse than being caught behind a shed because you can do anything you like in the bushes and the penalty for being caught is merciless. I want to take Mrs. Connor to the bushes.

"All right," I say.

Marianne runs to the bushes. She doesn't care about being caught. She doesn't care about anything. When I get there I am cold with the trembles because at last I am going to kiss Marianne Cameron. I wonder how I should start, maybe like Paul with my hand on her shoulder, but I don't get a chance to even think about it, Marianne kisses me full on the face and puts her tongue in my mouth. I push her away. It's disgusting.

"It's French kissing," she says. "Everyone does it."

"I don't."

"Because you don't know how. I'll show you."

"OK," I say. "But don't put your whole tongue in and not so quickly," I say.

She nods and she's gentle this time and it's nice, I suppose, but I still hate it and push her away. It's like eating ham.

"I don't like it," I say. "Can't we do it without your tongue?" I say.

"OK," she says.

"Lie back," I tell her.

She lies back. I get on top of her and put my lips on her lips and push really hard and move my head around like I've seen on the TV. She holds me tight but then she opens her mouth again and bites my top lip and I get off her then. It is sore and horrible. I'm very sad about the whole thing, to be honest. I always thought kissing Marianne Cameron would be the most amazing thing in the entire universe, but it isn't. She's like a big wet dog. I feel embarrassed.

"Michael," she says, "you want to see something?"

"OK," I say.

"But you can't tell anyone," she says.

"All right," I say.

She lifts up her skirts, pulls down her knickers, and shows me her fanny. I've seen a fanny before. Paul MacDonald has a collection of them in his gorgeous magazines with the beautiful women, but this is different, and so I run away and think Marianne Cameron is a terrible girl. I want to tell my da but I can't because then I would have to tell him about the bushes and the wet tongue and the wiggling about on top of Marianne Cameron and I don't think he should know about these things.

I go straight home instead and even though Granny has bought ice cream from the van, my very favorite, I go straight upstairs and put my pajamas on. I tell my da I am tired and don't feel well. Everyone believes me because I am never sick and they know it is serious because I like ice cream more than anything in the world and would do anything to eat it, except today. Ma checks my head and says it's a little warm. Da looks worried and Granny says she'll put the ice cream in the freezer for me.

"You can have it later," she says.

I turn on my side. I feel like crying. It is the worst day of my life.

fourteen

The war is over and a man called Simon Weston is badly wounded. He is burned all over his body and has no face. He is a hero and everyone loves him.

"It's a terrible thing not to have a face," says Da.

"It's a terrible thing to have two of them," laughs Granny.

Ma laughs hard, she's laughing more now, it's a miracle, but Da goes mental and slams his fists so hard on the table the cups filled with tea spill to the floor.

"Will no one talk about serious things in this house? Look at the man." He waves the paper in their faces. "He can't run from his troubles. He looks at them every day in the mirror and he doesn't turn away like a coward." He sits down, his face red with rage.

"What the fuck do you know about serious things?" says Ma. "You don't even have a job and you haven't even tried to find one."

"There are no jobs on this island!" yells Da.

"Then leave the fucking island. Go to the mainland. Travel on the boat every day. It's not hard, Brian."

"Not for you, Rosemary, with your bloody professor to keep you company."

"Not this again."

"I can't believe you told him," says Da. "Why would you do that? It's supposed to be a secret. We're going mad trying to keep it and you tell the first person that comes along. How could you do that to us?"

"Do what?"

"Tell a stranger."

"He's not a stranger to me," screams Ma.

She stomps out of the room, she's going anywhere to get away from Da, but he won't be left behind in the kitchen and follows her to the stairs. I don't know why everyone stomps everywhere in this house. It's a small house and there are only a few places you can go anyhow. There's the living room, the hall, or one of the bedrooms upstairs. Never the bathroom, which I think is a good place to go because it has a lock on the door.

"You think I don't know what's going on in Greenock, Rosemary, at your fancy college?" he yells. "I'm no fool."

I wonder what's going on in Greenock.

From the top of the stairs she yells, "Not a bloody thing. I'm learning and you can't stand it. He's my teacher."

"But why did you tell him?"

"I had no one else to tell," she screams.

"You said no one was to know and the shite I've had to put up with on account of it, it isn't fair. If you're going to tell people, then let's tell people here, let's tell the police. I can't take another evil eye. Even in church the pew is all mine, no fucker will sit near me because they think I bash my wife."

Granny can't send me anywhere because it's too late. I've already heard about the teacher and the secret Ma told him and I can't be sent out of the house because it's too dark and I can't be sent to my room because Ma and Da are fighting on the stairs and blocking the way to my bedroom.

"I felt someone else had to know. He won't say anything. He's a nice man. My work is suffering because of it. I don't want to fail this course. I can't fail. You'd like him. He's a nice man."

"Your fancy man. I don't think so."

"He's ready for retirement, you stupid bastard."

The room is silenced and Da really does feel like a stupid B-word.

"I'm sorry," he says. "I still think we need help with this. You're running around like a fart in a trance. You can't go on like this."

I laugh because saying "fart in a trance" is funny to me.

"Not in front of the boy, you two," says Granny.

They see me and smile. They feel bad. I'll get money out of this for sure.

"I know what I'm doing, Brian, but you have to trust me."

"I trust you, Rosemary, I worry for you. You can't blame a man for that."

Ma disappears into her room, where she keeps the special pills that help her sleep. I found them looking for my da's chewing gum. Ma told him his breath stinks and so he chews at it all day. For a minute I thought the pills were gum, a new kind, but Da was right behind me.

"What you looking for, Michael?"

"Some gum," I said.

"Here you go," said Da, lifting some from the table.

"Off you go," he said.

"What are these?" I said.

"Pills to help Ma get some shut-eye, to help us all get some shut-eye, but don't be touching them, all right? You'll get poisoned. They're not for children."

Da said Ma's teacher in Greenock helped her find them. Da was not pleased. He is afraid of men for Ma's sake, but since she sleeps without screaming now, he is also grateful, especially now he knows the teacher is old enough to marry my granny.

"It is a good thing for us all," said Granny. "Your ma has to sleep."

fifteen

Ma and Granny roll their eyes when it is the summer holidays. They never know what to do with me. Neither does Da. We don't go on holidays much. Other people do. They go to Butlin's or visit relatives in Glasgow and act like it's Mallorca or something. Some people actually go to Mallorca, like the McCabes. They love Mallorca and come back all brown and happy. Hairy McCabe is always showing off when she gets back about the fancy chewing gum you get in Spain, like we don't have chewing gum here in Scotland, but everyone always crowds round her like it's the best chewing gum the world has ever seen because it says "Chicle." Then she talks about the price and it's always really expensive, which makes her stupid for buying it as far as I'm concerned when she can get it for half the price at home, but it's always amazing to everyone how much the chewing gum costs in Mallorca. It's the same with Mars bars and Marathons, they cost pounds in Mallorca or so Hairy McCabe says. Mallorca is stupid. I like Rothesay best. We have beaches and every year the fair comes and we get goldfish. Mine always die after a few weeks but I don't mind because the next year I'll get a new one. I love the summer holidays, no one yelling at you to get out of bed, and it's always nice and warm except when it's raining and cold.

Also the talent show is soon, but I can hardly look at Marianne Cameron right now. She is a different girl to me. I tell no one about the bushes and neither does she, she would die of shame and I wouldn't blame her. What a show. Anyway, Dirty Alice would have said something if she knew and to everyone in the whole wide world most likely. Marianne acts like nothing has happened and sings even louder when I'm around. I try not to listen even when she's really good and makes people open their doors and sit on their steps peeling their potatoes or carrots. Sometimes Skinny Rab will bring a fag out and listen against the wall next to Marianne's ma. I wonder if they're still fighting like mad people.

Dirty Alice isn't saying much these days, which is a good thing because she's usually such a blabbermouth. Mr. McFadden and Mrs. Connor go everywhere together. It must make her sick with rage.

Da says it's nice to see Mr. McFadden looking so happy. Ma says the same and so does Granny. They like Mrs. Connor better these days since she has a regular man in her life with two children.

"She's turned herself around all right," says Ma.

"And seeing to that girl like she was her own daughter, which can't be easy with the lip she gets from her. Hair brushed. Shoes shined. Not so dirty anymore," says Granny.

She'll always be Dirty Alice to me, I think.

"She's a good woman. Haven't I been telling you that for years?" says Da.

Paul MacDonald's changed his tune too.

"I think Dirty Alice is looking all right now," he says to me.

"She's a dog," I say.

72

"She has nice long hair," says Fat Ralph.

Paul MacDonald is girl-mad but Fat Ralph isn't, not usually, and to notice Dirty Alice and her hair makes me angry and so I call him a poof.

"You want hair like Dirty Alice, don't you?" I say.

"No, I'm just saying it's long and shiny. What's wrong with having hair that's shiny?"

"Nothing, unless you want it for yourself," I say.

"I was just saying," says Ralph.

"Well, don't," I say.

It made me fairly annoyed Dirty Alice was being noticed at all, and I was upset at Fat Ralph because of all the people in the world he knows how much I hate Dirty Alice, even if her hair is shiny.

Fat Ralph and I are not as friendly as we used to be. He's hanging around with Paul, who's not dribbling in the talent show anymore. He's going to be bobbing about with Fat Ralph doing something stupid probably and they haven't asked me to bob about with them. I'm definitely not asking, so I hope they make an arse of themselves, maybe one of them will fall over and split his head open or something like that. I can do fifty keepy-uppies in two minutes without dropping one time. Ma is going to be so proud of me, so is Da and Granny.

Marianne has asked Tracey and Fiona to sing the song about the Japanese boy. This talent show is getting serious now and I'm wondering if it might actually happen. Tracey and Fiona have to wear their mas' housecoats and paint their faces white and use eyeliner like Mrs. Connor does on her eyes, all curly and dark. Tracey and Fiona are right excited. Marianne has also asked Dirty Alice to do the Highland fling. I don't understand why Marianne doesn't want to do everything anymore. She's great at everything. My ma says it's called "delegating" and Marianne is a clever girl to be sharing the responsibility.

"Singing every song will hurt her throat and be boring for everyone else. There are other girls that can sing around here. She's right to give them a chance," says Ma.

I think maybe I should sing with the boys, but I'd get laughed at and I don't like to be laughed at. I'll stick to the soccer ball. It's more manlike.

Anyway, Ma doesn't know anything about Marianne. I think she isn't singing all the songs because of Tricia Law. Marianne is sad and is afraid to sing probably. She knows we all know the scandal of her life and doesn't want us looking at her or something, except me, she let me look at her all right, but it was a different kind of looking. I hope she doesn't show it to anyone else because that would not be good for her reputation.

"Reputation is everything," says Granny.

sixteen

In the notices section of the local newspaper it says that Louisa Madeline Connor will marry Samuel John McFadden and that they're delighted to announce it. When Da sees Mr. McFadden he slaps him on the back and wishes him well. Ma and Granny give Mrs. Connor a hug, except she's not Mrs. Connor anymore and never was. She's Miss Connor.

"A Miss is someone who's not married. Connor was her maiden name, Michael," says Ma.

"So why does everyone call her Mrs. Connor?" I ask.

"No one does, only you. You call everyone Mrs.," says Ma.

"I do not," I say.

"It's an easy mistake to make. You're still young."

Telling me I am young annoys me. My ma thinks I'm a baby all the time. Anyway, they don't hate Miss Connor anymore, they call her Louisa because she's going to be a married woman, and she's not a slut anymore or a prostitute. Also there will be a big party at the Bowling Club everyone will go to. Granny and Ma like a good party, especially Granny because she gets to sneak a few brandies into her hip flask. That's what Da says, anyway.

Dirty Alice is furious about the whole thing. Everyone is a little afraid of Dirty Alice right now, everyone except me. I have beaten Paul MacDonald and I am the toughest lad in the world, but still, I don't want to be rolling around the grass with Dirty Alice McFadden to prove it. She broke a window and says "fuck" all the time; she also bit Fat Ralph on the leg. I bet he doesn't care about her shiny hair now. Da says she needs a good hiding. Ma says she needs to move on, and Granny says the whole family needs a priest to remove the angry spirit of Dirty Alice's ma, who is probably not keen on the wedding at all.

"She is probably up there not liking it one bit. The children need a mother but they also need a woman who goes to church, and Maria was nothing if she wasn't a good Catholic."

"Louisa's not a Catholic, Ma, she's divorced, so Maria up in heaven will have to lump it," says Da.

"I suppose she will. He has a mother for Alice and Luke, that's the main thing," says Granny.

"He's a lovely boy," says Ma.

Always on about Luke. I bet he'll be a bridesmaid.

Ma is in an especially good mood because she passed all her exams and she can now go on to the next level of her Open University course, which she is delighted about. Da has also decided to be delighted about it and doesn't care about the professor anymore and we all have a heavy cake Granny bakes to celebrate. Da gets indigestion because of it and Ma has a small piece so as not to offend Granny, who thinks she's a brilliant baker. Da says we have birds in the sky that wouldn't eat the crumbs in our garden. I have a big piece because I like the frosting. Granny makes nice frosting. It's not all bad with her baking.

Ma talks about going to university in Glasgow and though

Da balks at the idea, you can see Ma is serious and not to be stopped. She's like a train, but with all the sleep she gets at night Granny says it's a good thing and has improved her mood so we can all be happy, except Da, who is still sleeping on the sofa. He actually brings the lager home now, which he never did before. The cans have half-dressed women on the tin, I like to have a good look, but I keep getting caught by Ma or Granny and get slapped about the head. Now Da has to put a rag around his tin while he drinks, but I can still see their faces with the lovely red lipstick and the feet of their black stockings. They remind me of Miss Connor dancing in her living room, except with more clothes on. They do not remind me of Marianne. I don't know why that is and I have no one to ask about it, with Da busy with his beer and Ma busy with her learning. Granny isn't very busy at all but she'd most likely drag me to the priest or tell on Marianne and have her dragged to the priest, or worse, have her arrested for showing her fanny off.

I wish someone would arrest Dirty Alice; she wants to cancel the talent show and everything because she's in a bad mood. Everyone disagrees with her and is against her. She's got a long drippy face on her all the time because of this wedding. Even Luke is sick of it and actually opened his mouth to moan about her, which he never does.

"She's a terror in the house. Breaking things. Screaming. Da had to take the strap to her. Louisa cried the whole time, but I think Alice needed it. You know she broke my chess trophy?"

"No, I didn't. You must have been gutted, Luke," I say.

"Devastated," he says.

Then he went away, leaving us all stunned because he'd actually talked to us and that was a big surprise.

seventeen

The engagement party of Miss Connor and Mr. McFadden is a big scandal.

The party was at the Bowling Club and everyone was dressed up nice. They had punch for the children and punch for the grown-ups and my da loved that. Ma was so embarrassed by him because there was also a bar and he had pint after pint. The food was amazing. They had prawn cocktails, I love prawn cocktails, and everyone in the world does. And they had these little sticks with pineapple and cheese and little tiny onions rolled onto them. They also had sausage rolls and something called quiche I didn't like at all, but they had a lot of paste sandwiches and so I was as happy as a boy could be. They had a disco too with flashing lights, but only the women danced at first, with their handbags on the floor, and then some men danced around them, but the men were annoying the women I think and kept whispering in their ears. The women laughed at them, but then the men tried some more whispering and some of the ladies turned to dance with them. I wondered why Da didn't whisper to Ma and I wondered if Granny would stop drinking out of her hip flask when there was plenty of punch. I wondered a lot that night.

Marianne was there with her ma and da, and of course

Dirty Alice was wearing a nice dress because it was a special occasion; she actually looked clean for a change, but I didn't say anything. No way. Marianne made her dance and to all kinds of songs, but when Madness came on it was only the boys that got up to dance, not the grown-ups, they just watched us, and so we jumped up and down until the greatest song in the world was finished. It was the best of fun but I think all the mas and das were laughing at us, which wasn't right because we didn't laugh at them smooching about and whispering all over each other.

Then Tricia Law came in and wearing the shortest skirt anyone in the world had ever seen. Everyone started looking at Marianne's ma and Skinny Rab. He looked as scared as could be. He was back in the house and he had his family again, but Marianne's ma was still fuming because you could hear her shouting from the house sometimes. Marianne's ma looked like she wanted to kill Tricia Law.

"Jesus H," said Ma to Granny. They gave each other a terrible look, mostly because they were worried Tricia was going to cross the floor to where they were standing and they didn't want that because it would spoil the party, and make Marianne's ma think they were on Tricia's side. Ma went bright red, but Granny, who only likes Tricia a wee bit, went to the toilet hoping Ma would follow. But that's not what happened because before Tricia even got across the disco floor Marianne's ma took a wild run for her and pulled her to the ground like a big dog or something. People were pulling kids out of the way so they could get a better view of the fight. I got myself a chair. Marianne saw me and ran away. I suppose she didn't want me looking, but it was a fight, what was I supposed to do? I wanted to see Marianne's ma having a go at Tricia Law, who had been terrible to my da a lot of times. Da didn't care. He kept on drinking, even though Ma kept pulling at his sleeve to help out. Marianne's ma is a big lady and Tricia is very small but she was still a good fighter. There was a lot of slapping and pulling of hair because that's how girls fight. They also scream while they fight. They call each other nasty names. Boys just get on with it because we are better at fighting than girls. We have no time to talk or scream at each other. Also women cry before the fight is over, so it's hard to know who the winner is. There were lots of people trying to pull them apart and stop the scratching and biting, but Marianne's ma couldn't be pinned down. She was really strong and I bet Tricia was sorry she wore that short skirt because everyone saw her knickers. They were black like the girls' on the lager cans, but it wasn't a nice thing to see because she was fighting. Mr. McFadden was holding Miss Connor, who was crying because her party was spoiled. When Granny came out of the toilet she was sorry to have missed the scandal and also upset for Miss Connor.

Paul and Fat Ralph were also standing on chairs; to be honest we were having a good time watching Marianne's ma going at Tricia Law like that. Paul would talk about Tricia's knickers for a long time. I would not because I know her and it's not right to look at the knickers of someone who comes to your house and drinks tea with your ma.

The fight was eventually stopped by Da and Skinny Rab. Skinny Rab was holding back Marianne's ma with all his strength and Da was holding back Tricia.

"Ladies, enough," said Da.

"She fucked my husband," screamed Marianne's ma.

80

"Maybe if you had fucked him yourself he wouldn't have come running to me," said Tricia.

Marianne's ma went to take a run at her again but Skinny Rab had a good hold of her.

Tricia fell into my da's arms like a swooning princess and started crying, and Marianne's ma buried her head into Skinny Rab's shoulder and started punching at his arm.

"Why? Why her?" she yelled and in front of everyone in the town.

He grabbed at her wrists and said sorry a hundred times and then he pulled Marianne's ma away from the fighting.

"Come on, love," whispered Skinny Rab.

Ma came to help Da with Tricia and to give her a coat to hide her knickers from everyone.

About ten minutes later Skinny Rab came in shouting for Marianne.

"Marianne, Marianne. Have you seen Marianne, Brian?"

He went on like that for ages until other people started looking for Marianne too, except Tricia Law, who was sipping brandy from my granny's hip flask. She didn't care where Marianne was.

Da said it was time for us all to go but then the police showed up and we thought they were going to arrest Tricia and her black knickers, but they didn't, they were looking for Marianne like everyone else was.

"I haven't seen her," I say.

"Where's the last place you did see her?" says Mr. MacLeod. Mr. MacLeod is a very fat policeman. Da says he couldn't catch a turtle, never mind a criminal.

"He'd have a heart attack," said Da one time.

This made everyone laugh, including Ma. Da was very funny to her once.

"Where does she like to go?" says Mr. MacLeod.

"I don't know. The Woody," I say.

"She's not in the Woody, we looked there already," says Mr. MacLeod.

"Maybe the park," says Dirty Alice, who is standing behind me and gives me a little bit of a fright.

"It's pitch black. She'd never go there. She's a cowardy custard of the dark," I say.

"How do you know?" Dirty Alice nips, and then she pushes me and in front of everyone. I hate her.

"All girls are scared of the dark," I shout.

"That's enough, you two," snaps Da, who has gone as white as a sheet. Ma looks like she's about to burst into tears and Granny takes a nip of the brandy. They are thinking the flasher has her.

"Do you know where she is, Alice?" asks Mr. MacLeod.

Dirty Alice goes as red as a berry.

"Alice, if you know where Marianne is, you have to tell us," says Ma. "Did she go to the park?"

Dirty Alice shrugs.

Ma grabs her. "Where did she go?" She actually shakes her. Ma's scared.

"I'll handle this, Rosemary," says Mr. MacLeod, and then he grabs Alice by the shoulders and shakes her exactly like Ma did.

"Where is she?" he yells.

Dirty Alice starts to cry and no wonder with all the shaking she's getting. I don't feel bad for her though, everyone hates her now and she deserves it.

"She's under my bed," says Dirty Alice.

"Under your bed?" says Granny. "What the hell is she doing under your bed, lassie?"

"Hiding from all of you!"

Dirty Alice runs away.

"Go get her," says Da.

"No," I say.

"Do as you're told!" says Ma. "Brian, take Tricia home."

Da looks like he doesn't want to.

"Do it," says Ma.

Da pulls a terrible face but leaves with Tricia anyway. I am made to chase stupid Dirty Alice, even though I don't care if she gets lost.

Everyone else runs away to tell Skinny Rab and Marianne's ma that Marianne is safe under the bed of Dirty Alice, which I bet is filthy.

When I get outside I find Miss Connor hugging Dirty Alice with Mr. McFadden. Mr. McFadden is telling her everything is OK and doesn't seem to mind that Marianne is hiding in his house under the disgusting bed of Dirty Alice, getting poisoned probably. I go back inside. There is no one there except Fat Ralph and he's stuffing his face with paste sandwiches and there's the lovely pink cake that won't get eaten, but then Miss Connor comes in and asks us if we want a slice and cuts it all up for us to eat. People start to come back inside after a while and someone starts up the music again, but it's not a party anymore. Everyone is talking about the fight and eating mostly. People love to eat and talk. Miss Connor and Mr. McFadden don't care though and when the slushy music comes on they dance and are happy again. I wish Ma and Da would dance like that but Da has taken Tricia home and Ma is eating cake alone. Granny yawns and wants to go home in a taxi, but I want to stay and eat the cake that I nearly choke on when I see Paul MacDonald dancing with Dirty Alice as if they like each other. It's a horrible thing to watch and when I see Paul in the morning I will tear into him for being so stupid, dancing with a dog like Dirty Alice.

When we get home Ma and Granny are shocked to find Tricia Law sleeping on our sofa.

Da is watching TV, drinking a cup of tea.

"What the hell is she doing here?" gasps Ma.

"I don't know where she lives, do I?"

"The Brae," says Granny. "We went there New Year's. Are you stupid? Now get going. I'll not be waking to that sight in the morning."

"I'm not dragging Tricia Law with her knickers about her ankles up any Brae. Not everyone was at that party. They'd think all sorts of things."

"Just leave her," says Ma to Granny.

I wondered where Da would sleep that night and was glad Tricia Law got a hiding from Marianne's ma. She'd taken Da's bed and made Marianne run away. She was not a nice lady to me and her knickers are stupid. I hope she catches her death of cold.

eighteen

The flasher is at it again. This time a fifteen-year-old girl at the Academy, but he doesn't catch her. She ran away like Ma did. It was in the local paper, but we're not to know her name because the victim is so young, but everyone knows it was Suzanne Miller, who is a cashier in the supermarket on Saturdays.

"She is a good runner and plays hockey," says Paul. "He must have been scared to death of her."

I want to tell them my ma is a good runner also, but I don't. They can't know a thing about Ma and the flasher. In the morning I am told again to keep my gob shut.

"It's more important than ever, Michael. Not one word," says Da.

"Not one," repeats Granny.

Suzanne Miller is a big hero in the town now and when we go to the supermarket she is working her till as usual. She doesn't look like Ma did when she was flashed. Suzanne's face is normal and bright. She has no bruises or cuts. No scars or bleeding from her head. Granny deliberately stands in line for Suzanne's till, I know this because there are three other tills she could easily go to and all she has is a loaf of bread in her basket.

When I look behind me I see lots of women and men lining up behind Granny, all of them wanting to know the story of the flasher and how Suzanne escaped a terrible pervert. When Granny gets her turn, she tells Suzanne what a brave girl she is, getting away from a monster like that. Suzanne is excited and can't wait to tell us the story.

"Oh, Mrs. Murray, I was frightened for my life. He grabbed at me like this."

Suzanne shows us how he grabbed her and puts her own arms across her throat. "And he was trying to drag me like this." She tips her head back and steps back a little. I wonder about Ma being dragged before he showed her his willy and she ran away. My poor ma, she must have been so scared.

"He was trying to pull me into the Glen you see. Can you imagine if he'd gotten me in there?" says Suzanne.

"Doesn't bear thinking about," says Granny.

Suzanne whispers, "He could have raped me, Mrs. Murray."

Granny is stone cold. I wonder what rape is and I am going to ask when Granny puts her hand across my mouth.

"Sorry, Mrs. Murray. I didn't see him there," says Suzanne.

"How did you get away from him?" asks Granny.

"Well, when he tried to pull me into the Glen he tripped back into the stump of a tree, didn't he? Fell on his arse, so I started running. Screaming I was."

"Did he show you his willy?" I ask.

Granny slaps me across the head.

"How dare you ask a question like that, you filthy wee beggar. Say sorry to Suzanne."

"S'all right," says Suzanne. "They're bound to be curious at that age, aren't they? And no, Michael, he showed me no such thing."

"Did you see his face, Suzanne? Did you notice anything about him at all?" whispers Granny.

She shakes her head. "He came from behind me, didn't he? But did I mention his chain? He had a gold one on his wrist, that's all I remember. I couldn't help the police at all."

When we get out of the supermarket Granny is dragging me home and I know I am going to get the tanning of my life, just for asking about willies, but that's not what happens. I am sent to bed early, but I can't sleep. I can hear shouting from downstairs.

"The boy should know," says Da. "He's already asking questions. He's not stupid. He knows it's something."

Ma screams, "He's not to know."

Granny says, "I agree with Rosemary. The boy thinks it was a flasher. Let him think that is what it was. It's safer that way."

It wasn't a flasher, I think to myself, and I am shocked to my bones.

"Suzanne Miller was almost raped. Are you both mad? We can't keep this to ourselves any longer."

"It's Rosemary's business," says Granny to Da.

"Someone else will get hurt. Do you want that on your conscience, Rosemary?" Da screams.

"I can't," cries Ma.

"We'll go to the police. They'll understand," says Da.

"It's too late," says Granny. "They'd never believe her."

"Would you shut your mouth?" screams Da.

"Don't you talk to me like that!" cries Granny.

"Then stop talking shite," says Da.

"I don't want to. I won't. And if you want to stay married to me, Brian Murray, you won't mention this again," growls Ma.

"But you told your professor. Telling the police will be exactly the same."

"That was different. My teacher is not from here. You know how they are in this town. They'd say terrible things. They'd say I took him to the park," cries Ma. "He didn't do to Suzanne what he did to me."

"That girl was saved by God," says Granny, but Granny says that about everything, especially food that's fallen on the floor.

"He'll have got a scare now, Brian. He won't do it again. I know he won't," yells Ma.

"You know nothing of the kind," cries Da. "None of us do. He'll do it again and shame on all of us if he does."

Da slams the kitchen door. I hear a shuffle around the coat stand and the front door slam closed. Da doesn't care he's not welcome in the pubs. He doesn't care people will make remarks about him beating up his wife and he doesn't care no one will sit next to him. Da is going for a pint. He is going for lots of pints but he won't bring chips home. He'll bring bruises and words he shouldn't say and then he'll fall asleep on the concrete steps until Granny and Ma drag him to his feet and take him to the sofa. Ma will put a cover on him and want to kiss his forehead, but she won't. She'll cry and Granny will comfort her. Ma will go to her room and take her pills and she will fall asleep. Granny will make a cup of tea and I will sneak down beside her. She puts her arms around my shoulder.

"You want some hot chocolate, son?" she says.

"Yes, please," I say, even though it's watery, it's still choco-late. After a while Granny cries. I put my arm around her. I feel bad because she wants to tell me all about rape but can't, but like Da says, I'm going to find out about it sooner or later and when I do it's going to make everyone angry.

nineteen

I get to eat cornflakes every morning for breakfast when it's the holidays. I scatter tons of sugar all over them and mix them with loads of cold milk. In wintertime I have to have warm milk, or worse, porridge.

"Would you look at that?" says Da, waving the paper about. "Some fucker broke into the Queen's own bedroom and asked for a fag."

"Would you watch your language in front of the lad?" says Ma, even though Ma says worse words in front of me. Ma slams down the shirt she's mending and leaves the room. Da doesn't care. He doesn't even look round. He is used to Ma and her nippy ways. We all are.

"Scaled the wall in his bare feet and no one saw a thing," says Da.

"Let me see that," says Granny and pores over Da's shoulder. It annoys him because he starts to squirm around. He doesn't like his ma too close to him.

"Poor Elizabeth," says Granny. "She must have been scared shitless. Thank God for her butler."

Da sniggers at this and I snigger too, I think it's funny that a butler saves the day and so does Da. Da gives me a big smile and then it falls quickly from his face like all Da's smiles do these days.

I think of what Suzanne was whispering in the supermarket. *"Could have raped me, Mrs. Murray,"* and I feel a chill go down my back. It's a bad word for sure and saying it to anyone would most likely get me tanned. It sounds like *rip* and I wonder if they're sort of the same. There are so many words I'm not meant to know or say, even though everyone else says them, like *shitless* and *fucker* and *bastard*. They must be stupid if they think I don't know what those words mean, but here is a word I don't know, and the word is *rape* and so I borrow Ma's dictionary and get a pen and a piece of paper to write everything down. I know it's going to be a big thing when I read about it. I find the word quickly.

Rape, raped, raping. *Force of a man or other persons to have sexual intercourse by the threat or use of violence against any person.*

Force, I think. *Violence*.

I think I know about *intercourse* because Paul MacDonald told me after Deirdra was screaming about it in class one time. I think there is something wrong with Deirdra. Granny says she is a bit touched in the head.

Anyway, Paul got his nudie magazines out and told me intercourse was when a man gets hard in his willy and gets naked with one of the women in the pictures showing their fannies off. I know Ma would never show her fanny to anyone and it makes me feel scared. I ask him again, even though I know he will tear lumps out of me.

"Are you stupid or something? I told you already. Intercourse is like shagging and doing wanking, it's all the same, but you have to do it with a woman. My da told me."

I am suddenly worried Paul and his da have made a mistake and so I look up *intercourse* again.

Intercourse. *Communications between individuals or groups of persons or coitus.*

I am more confused than ever and flick through the pages until I am at C. I eventually find *coitus.*

Coitus. *Sexual intercourse.*

I am running in circles, everything means the same, and so I look up *sexual* again.

Sexual. *Pertaining to or involving sexual relations.*

I am suddenly not sure about anything and decide to ask Da about all the words, except *rape*, but I wait till Ma and Granny are doing something else, but then Granny walks in and hears me ask about the word *sexual* and gets very angry with me. Ma is right behind her and there I am, stuck with all of them and not wanting to know any words at all.

"*Sexual* is not a word I want to hear uttered in this house," says Granny.

"Away and shite, woman," says Da. "They're perfectly normal words for any growing lad to know."

I blame Paul MacDonald and tell them he said them in the car park. I don't tell them about the dirty magazines because they would tell his ma and da and the magazines would be taken away and I like the magazines. Anyway Granny said *sexual* was a sinful word but was not surprised it was used in Paul MacDonald's house with "*those sisters running around.*" Paul has three of them, and except for Georgina, the rest of his sisters look a lot like Paul, which is a shame because they're very nice girls, even though they get about a bit. That's what Granny says anyway, but she says that about a lot of people. If she knew about Marianne and her fanny, she would say worse about her and probably tell her ma.

Anyway, Da says it's human to be sexual and have intercourse.

"It's about reproduction and a whole bunch of other stuff. Evolution, son."

"Is it about being naked, Da?" I ask.

"Sometimes," says Da.

Granny crosses herself.

"Is it the same as coitus, Da?"

"'Coitus,'" laughs Da. "Where did you hear a word like that?"

I want to tell him about *rape* and the dictionary but I can't.

"For the love of God, would you make him stop with all these questions?" says Granny, who is making a big horrible cake for after dinner and stirring the batter quickly. I wonder what she puts in her cakes to make them hurt your chest so bad when you swallow them. I decide I won't eat one bite.

Da ignores Granny and Ma says nothing at all.

"Sometimes you have to be naked and sometimes you don't and sometimes it's about intercourse, *or coitus*, you know, when a man and a woman lie down together, it's hard to explain, Michael, so let's leave it alone before Granny here has a fit in the kitchen."

"But is sexual intercourse and coitus the same as sex, Da?" I ask.

"Yes," says Da. He's getting annoyed now, so I let it alone and go back to my dictionary. I check all the words again until

I get to *force*, which I know is making people do things they don't want to, and *violence*, when you smack people. I flick back to *rape*.

Rape, raped, raping. *Force of a man or other persons to have sexual intercourse by the threat or use of violence against any person.*

Force, I think. *Violence. Sexual intercourse. Violence. Force.*

Ma's blood, I think.

Ma's cuts.

Ma's tears.

Ma!

twenty

Every summer Granny drags us to the top of Barone Hill next to the graveyard to pick wild raspberries for her jam. She makes sandwiches, a flask of hot tea (even though it's boiling outside), and scones. Da brings his paper and a bottle of fizzy juice. It's a weird day for fizzy juice, we only get fizzy juice when the sun is out, and today there is no sun, it's just a really hot day, the kind that makes you sweat and feel funny when you breathe.

"It's clammy," says Granny.

On berry-picking day Ma is in good form but I feel strange around her now. I make mistakes around her, like walking into her room for chewing gum and catching her getting dressed.

"What are you standing there for?" she says.

"Looking for Juicy Fruit," I say.

"Then look for Juicy Fruit and stop looking at me," she nips.

I grab for the Juicy Fruit and look to the floor but it makes me bang into the edge of the door and I hurt my head.

"Now you'll get a bruise," she says and comes to look at my face. She looks up close and I can smell her breath. I hate it and want to run for my life. I squirm away from her. I want to leave with my Juicy Fruit.

"What's the matter, Michael?" she whispers.

"Nothing," I say.

She shakes her head and sighs. "Do you want to talk about something?" she asks.

"No!" I say. "I want to go downstairs."

It's terrible to know too many things about people. It makes you feel like a liar because you have to act like you know nothing at all when the truth is you know everything there is to know.

Ma would hate it if she thought I knew, and if I gave her a hug or something and said I was sorry about the man in the park she would probably go mad with tears and never sleep again.

"I don't want to go berry-picking," I tell her, trying to think of something to say.

"What are you talking about? You love berry-picking," says Ma and strokes my head.

"It's too hot," I say.

"Then wear a T-shirt," she chirps.

"I don't have one," I say.

In her tights and shirt she goes to my bedroom and I just wish she would put the rest of her clothes on.

"Here," says Ma and reaches into a drawer and pulls out my Celtic top.

"That's my good shirt. I don't want to waste it berry-picking. It'll get juice on it," I say.

"Then this," says Ma, throwing another shirt at me, not a good shirt, but still not one to be ruined berry-picking.

"Would you stop throwing my clothes around?" I say and

with a lot of cheek in me too, but she doesn't even get mad. She just rolls her eyes to heaven.

"I'm away to get dressed, Michael," she smiles. "Find yourself a shirt and I'll meet you downstairs."

I find an old yellow T-shirt with a tomato-sauce stain on the shoulder. It's a bit small but I don't mind, it can get wasted to death for all I care. It's a rubbish T-shirt. I hate it. I hope a whole basket of berries ruins it and I can throw it in the bin.

"What's that you're wearing, Michael?" says Granny.

"What does it look like?" I say.

"It's too small, go take it off," says Granny. "The neighbors will think we don't dress you right."

"If he wants to wear it let the lad alone. It's not a wedding we're going to," says Ma and gives me a wink. It makes me smile, although it's hard to smile at her with all I know.

Even though Ma is being nice, I hate we're going berry-picking together. It makes me feel sick in my stomach, but not like I could throw up, a different kind of sick, like swirls and knots.

Da yells for Frankie, who goes crazy with excitement. Frankie loves going anywhere with Da. He goes mad and jumps all over the place and that means Da can't get the lead on him and has to shout at him to sit down; this makes Frankie pee himself with worry and makes Granny all angry. I love Frankie for peeing but he can be a bit stupid about it.

"He has too many emotions, that dog," says Da but pats him anyway.

Poor Frankie, he has no idea where he's going because he's a dog and he's never been berry-picking before. It's boring, I want to tell him. I bet they tie him up somewhere, on a lamp-post probably, and he will boil to death. Da takes a wee bowl for him just in case.

"What's that for?" says Granny.

"It's roasting outside. He'll get thirsty," says Da. "I'll nip up the graveyard and use the sink."

"That water is for the dead," says Granny.

"I'm sure they won't be missing it, Shirley," says Ma. She smiles at Da. Da gives her a wink and then they look at me to take part in the teasing of Granny, but I don't join in and ignore them.

"It's for the flowers of the departed," whispers Granny.

"God won't mind if we give wee Frankie here a dram of water," says Da.

Granny pulls a face because Da will go to the graveyard anyway.

Getting to the berry patch means walking through the entire housing estate and I feel stupid wearing the yellow T-shirt all of a sudden and hope no one sees me, but everyone sees me and I'm holding two baskets like a girl. Granny made me.

Dirty Alice and Marianne see me, but they don't say anything because Granny would give them a right telling-off. Also Marianne would be scared I'd tell everyone she showed me her fanny. Then I see Aidan Greer and he says nothing either because he knows I'll kick his arse next time I see him if he does.

Ma looks good swinging a basket, she looks happy. The scars are healed on her face, although you can still see a little red ripple above the left side of her lip. I should be glad she can smile again but I know inside she is still sad. I don't like the sad inside her. I'm scared of it. I remember how it screamed about the place and couldn't sleep.

I wonder about the other night when Tricia came over and talked like mad about Suzanne Miller. Tricia said it was all people were talking about. Granny didn't even look up from her tea and now I know why.

"The community center is running self-defense classes so we can kick the shit out of anyone trying to attack us," said Tricia, smoking.

"Wouldn't help," Ma said to her.

"It would fucking help me. I'd fight to the death," she told Ma. I know now this must have made Ma feel horrible, as if she didn't fight him enough when he hurt her in the park.

"If a big man came at you, Tricia, you would turn to water and the only thing you would be thinking is 'Don't kill me.' You wouldn't be fighting anyone." Granny finished her cigarette and put the kettle on for more tea.

"Well, all the women on this island are terrified and all the men are walking them everywhere for safety. It's some big thing in town."

I wonder how bad my ma must have felt about her saying that and I start to hate Tricia all over again.

So many things start to make sense to me now and it makes me mad. I thought I was the one keeping a big secret for them about a stupid flasher when all the time they were the ones keeping a big secret from me.

"Rosemary is doing well," says Granny to Da one night but that was before I knew what they were talking about.

"Be better if she could sleep without the pills," says Da.

"What do you want from the girl?" snips Granny. "After what she's been through, it's a wonder she hasn't downed the whole bottle."

"What a thing to say, Ma," says Da.

"It's the truth. She's got strength and if I didn't know better I'd say you were scared of it," says Granny.

Granny says all kinds of things to Da and I wonder how he can stand it, she can be fairly rude, but Da can be rude back. I can't be anything to Granny or I'd get skelped. I wonder if it was like this when Da was wee. I wonder what kind of things he dared to say to Granny then. I bet he didn't say a word, but now he says a ton of them.

We pick berries until my arms are sick of being scratched.

"Are we done yet?" I ask.

"Nearly done," says Ma.

"We should go soon," says Da. "I don't like the look of those clouds."

Ma picks loads of berries but she also keeps eating them and it drives Granny mad.

"You'll get a gut ache if you're not careful, Rosemary," Granny says. Ma rolls her eyes to heaven.

Da hardly picks any. He just sits on a patch of lazy grass with Frankie and reads his paper. One time he goes to the graveyard to get the water and Granny is furious and then the rain comes.

"Here it comes," says Da. "Let's get going."

It starts to thunder in the distance and then clouds start to spit at us.

That's when Granny sees the car. A hearse. Long and black and with other cars trailing behind it.

"Oh Jesus. A funeral. That's all we need and here we are picking berries and stealing dead people's water. It's a cursed day."

"Only for the poor sod in the hearse," says Da.

"What an awful thing to say to your mother," says Granny.

As the cars roll by, Da waves at a few faces he recognizes, so does Ma and on the other side of the road Granny does the same.

"Elsa Chapman it was," says Granny on the way home.

"Who's Elsa Chapman?"

"Mary Chapman's older sister. I never knew her. She lived off the island, moved to Canada. I think her husband died and she came back to be near family."

"We saw Malcolm and Sheila," says Da.

"I saw Vera and Hale," says Granny. She crosses herself and then I cross myself and smile at her knowing Granny will be thrilled to pieces. It was just for fun really.

"What the hell was that, Michael?" says Ma.

"I was crossing myself like Granny does."

Granny kisses the top of my head and gives Ma a triumphant look. "This lad needs to be baptized," says Granny.

"*Away 'n' shite*, Shirley, he needs nothing more than a few drama classes."

"Just because the boy shows a healthy interest in his own religion doesn't mean we need to send him to the Fame Academy," nips Da.

"What do you care for religion? You were drinking from the well of the dead a minute ago," says Ma.

"It's just water, for God's sake. I agree with Ma. Michael crossed himself, it's time we took him to church," says Da.

I am suddenly wishing I hadn't crossed myself at all. I was just playing a joke on Granny and now I know it wasn't funny.

"I suppose you mean your church?" Ma says.

"You don't have a church, Ma," I say.

"You're not a Catholic, Michael, trust me, you'll thank me for it one day," says Ma.

"Maybe I want to go to church. Maybe I want to go with Da," I yell.

Ma is fuming and more than usual. Granny starts to cry with joy.

"You can shut those fucking tears off, Shirley. You've been turning that boy ever since you came into my house. Well, I'm not having it," says Ma.

"Don't you talk to my mother like that," yells Da.

That's when Ma throws the berries away. Everyone on the street, anyone fixing their car, kids playing with other kids, everyone can hear the commotion.

"It's all right, Ma, I won't go to church," I say, but Ma has walked off and no one can catch up to her. Da doesn't want to anyway. I help Granny and Da pick the berries from the road. Ma's went and ruined the day and just because I was having a bit of fun with Granny. I didn't know she'd get so serious over it. It makes me annoyed at her.

When we get home Ma is in the kitchen and she has a suitcase at her side.

"Michael, go to your room," says Ma.

"Stay right where you are, son," says Da.

"Jesus, Rosemary, if you feel that strongly about it," sighs Granny.

"It's not that, it's all of you. I can't stay here anymore," cries Ma.

"Is it because I crossed myself?" I ask.

"No, Michael, it's not because of you. It's everything. I can't take it anymore," says Ma. She sounds sort of wobbly in her voice and she doesn't look anyone in the eye.

"Rosemary, are you all right?" whispers Da.

"I have a friend in Greenock who says I can stay with her," says Ma.

I can hardly breathe.

"Ma, I won't go to church. I swear I won't. I was just playing around," I say.

"It's not about the church, Michael. I have to get out of here. Please understand," cries Ma.

"Is it because you were raped?" I spit.

The room stills. Ma whitens.

"Who have you been talking to?" says Ma.

"No one," I cry.

She suddenly grabs at my shoulders.

"I said, who have you been talking to?" she yells.

"You're hurting me," I scream.

"Let him go," cries Da.

"I'm sorry, Ma, I'm sorry."

She slaps me. Everything sharpens. She slaps me again.

"Rosemary," cries Da and pulls her away from me. She slides to the floor and cries out.

"I'm sorry," she says. "I'm sorry."

I reach for my ma and I hold her tight, but she won't put her arms around me.

"You're not supposed to know," she cries. "You're not supposed to know."

"Ma," I cry.

"Get him away from me," she screams.

She doesn't want me. My ma doesn't want me. She starts banging her fists into the floor. My ma is hurting herself.

"I'm calling the doctor," says Da. Granny nods.

I run to my room. I don't want to see what happens next. I don't want to hear any more words or screams. I don't want to see my ma hate me.

After the doorbell rings there is a rumble of voices and it goes on for a long time. I know it is over when my da comes into my room. I have turned the lights out.

"Michael," he says.

I am pretending I am asleep, but it is my da and I can't lie to him.

"Is Ma all right?" I ask.

"She's not herself, Michael, because of the rape."

"It's a terrible thing to have happened to my ma," I cry.

"Who told you?" asks Da.

"I guessed," I say. Even though I needed my dictionary, even though they lied.

"I'm sorry he got my ma," I say.

"Me too," he says.

"Will they catch him, Da?" I say.

"I hope to God they do," says Da.

"What about Ma?" I ask.

"The doctor gave her something and she's asleep now," says Da.

"We have to tell the truth, Da," I say.

"We can't. No one in this town can know the truth. Can you do that for your ma, Michael? Can you keep a secret?" says Da.

I nod my head. I am the best at keeping secrets in the whole town. I am better than James Bond.

"It's not your fault, son, and I'm glad you know," says Da.

"Does Ma not like me anymore?" I ask.

"Don't be stupid, Michael. She's your ma and she will love you all her days," says Da.

"Can I make her something nice?" I say.

"Like what?"

"A key holder. I'm making one in school," I say.

"A key holder would be lovely," says Da.

I can tell Da doesn't want to leave. I don't know what he's going to do and so I just make ready to sleep. I am not at all surprised when he lies next to me. I expect him to. He is very sad, sadder than I have ever seen him. He sleeps before I do. I don't like the smell of his breath. It doesn't smell of beer but something else. It is a strong smell and it came from the bottle in the larder where Granny keeps the giant bags of flour and sugar. Granny hides it there and then shakes her head when Da pours from it.

"It's the hard stuff he's after now," says Granny. I know she means vodka and whiskey.

My da is sad, my granny is sad. We are all afraid and I pray for my ma to get better.

twenty-one

Ma has new medicines and they make her feel better. She is quiet. Everyone is quiet.

No one says, "Not in front of the boy" anymore, and I get to listen to anything I want these days, so long as I am silent and make them forget I am standing there, but it's not as good as spying. I liked to spy. I always knew stuff they didn't want me to know and it made me feel good.

Last week in the kitchen Granny started in with the crying. I was standing outside the door and glad to be, I hate to hear the crying, you mostly have to be quiet when people cry and it's all everyone does in this house. I am lucky I don't live in a swimming pool.

"What's the matter, Ma?" says Da.

"The gossip, Brian. I can't stand it. They think all kinds of things about you and Rosemary."

"They'll find something new to talk about in no time."

"They still think you did something to her, you know. They think you're a hard man in your house and hurt your family in some way."

"Let them think what they want," says Da. "The important thing is Rosemary is getting on and feeling better again. It's all that matters to me."

"Do you still think she wants to leave us?" Granny asks.

That's when I get caught by Ma, hovering at the kitchen door.

"You going in or out, Michael?" she asks.

"In," I say.

Ma goes over to Da and kisses his head.

"I never wanted to leave, Shirley. I didn't know what I was saying," says Ma.

Da goes as red as a berry but you can tell he's thrilled to bits he's had a wee peck from Ma. Ma pours herself a cup of tea at the stove and helps herself to Granny's fags; she hasn't done this in a long time and we are all shocked to death. The Wally dogs will just have to go yellow again.

Tricia Law still comes to the house, and though she is quiet with Da, she is always pleased to see Ma. Ma is still strange with me but has started smiling and says she is coming to the talent show, but I think the talent show might be ruined now and it will be Christmas before anyone gets to sing anything. School has already started and Halloween is around the corner and who wants to sit on their arses freezing to death watching kids singing and dancing?

Da and I took Frankie for a walk round the loch last week and Ma came behind us in her big coat with the furry hood. She looks good, but she still has the sadness in her eyes, I don't think it will ever go away, maybe it isn't supposed to. It was nice she came with us though. Da was really happy. He gave her Frankie's lead to hold and we went round the loch. I didn't say too much but she asked me a lot of questions about school and Halloween. What I was going to dress up in and so on. I told her a soldier. She smiled. She must love soldiers. Da said I should go as Rambo.

"He'd freeze to death being Rambo; the man doesn't have a stitch on him. A soldier is ideal. I'll get you a cap from the mainland."

"I'll give you the money, Rosemary."

Ma loves it when Da is generous with his cash. I think she thinks it means he loves her more or something. Sometimes when I share my sweets from the van people think you're really nice, but you only give your sweets if the person you are sharing with promises to share their sweets when they get money. If you don't, there are fights and long faces and terrible grudges. Granny only gives to family. "Never a lender or a borrower be," says Granny.

"She's right," says Da. "Family first, remember that, Michael."

Dirty Alice always has money for the van because Miss Connor always gives it to her. She's not so dirty these days either and I might change her name to Alice again, but I'm only thinking about it; she still falls about all over the place making herself dirty sometimes. Ma says Alice is a magnet for filth, but she's getting better and nicer these days. She gave me some penny dainties last week, just offered them and for no reason whatsoever. "Do you want some dainties, Michael?" she said. For a minute I thought she might have licked them and put the wrappers back on or something disgusting like that, but they looked brand-new and so I took them and said thank you, though it was a big surprise. She even said "See you later" and bounced back home. I was shocked to death.

Dirty Alice's da and Miss Connor are getting married soon and Dirty Alice has had to clean her act up because she is to be a bridesmaid. Luke is to be the best man and Da has been asked to be an usher. He was so pleased. I don't think Mr. Mc-Fadden has many friends. Neither does Miss Connor but they have relatives from far away. That's what Granny says.

"It's going to be a big thing," says Granny, who has already seen the dress and is pulling it in a bit at the back for Miss Connor, who wants to be the most beautiful bride there ever was.

"She's as skinny as a rake that one, you could play a tune on her rib cage," says Granny. "It's going to be some amount of work, this dress," but that's what Granny always says when she does favors for people so they are more thankful; Granny loves it when people are thankful.

Tricia Law is not invited because of the show she put on at the engagement party. This pleased Marianne's ma and she gave Miss Connor a beautiful tea set as a wedding present.

"Very expensive," says Granny. "Very expensive."

"Amounted to a pretty penny for Rab, no doubt, but that's the cost of shame," says Da.

"Rab's a bastard. He told Tricia a lot of lies, made promises he shouldn't have. There's more to the story than meets the eye," says Ma.

"You're probably right, Rosemary," says Da and gives her a nice smile. They agree about lots of things these days and Da is fixing up the garden just like he promised.

It was a nice day to be taking Frankie for a walk, a bit cold, but it was a fresh cold and you could breathe in nice air and smell the lovely flowers. I wanted to pick one for Ma but it would have been daft and she might not have liked it really. She might have thought I was doing it because of what happened in the park.

"Do you want to hold the dog, Michael?" says Ma.

"Sure, Ma. Are you tired?" I say.

"A little bit," says Ma.

And then she takes Da's arm. He took it no problem. It was a miracle. Granny says she is taking new pills now, not sleeping pills, but pills to cheer her up. Granny says Ma is still fragile.

"She is depressed, Michael, and it is a terrible thing to be depressed. You're not to tell anyone," says Granny.

I sigh. More secrets, I think. I'm getting tired of them, but I'm glad the pills make Ma want to be nice to Da again and maybe me.

Halfway round the loch Da does a funny thing: he suggests we walk back the way we came. This is not what we usually do but then I remember the park and how we have to pass it by and so does Ma. I see the gloom cross her face, just like it did when we were berry-picking. I think she is going to shout at us all and stomp off to somewhere and pack up her bags to Greenock again, but she doesn't, she turns to Da and says, "I think that's a good idea, Brian," and so we turn around and go back home all topsy-turvy. Da takes Ma's arm and promises to take me fishing again, but he never will.

Later in the day we go home for our dinner and Granny makes a big thing with sausages and eggs and bacon and fried bread. It's my favorite breakfast and to have it for dinner is very special. I like to have a cup of tea with it and Granny wants to use the china cups and so I am sent to the cabinet in the living room. I have to be quiet though because Ma is having a nap. The curtains in the front room are closed and the room is dark. I don't make a sound but Ma does.

"Michael," she whispers.

"Yes, Ma. Did I wake you? I'm sorry," I say.

"Don't be sorry," she says.

I get the cups.

"Michael," she says again. "Sit with me for a minute."

And so I sit at the bottom of the sofa, but I don't want to.

"You know I never meant to hurt you that time," she says.

"I know, Ma. You were not yourself," I say. "Da told me. Can I go now?"

"In a minute," she says. "You know, Michael, right now I'm in a bad way, but I'll get better, I promise," she says.

I nod because I don't know what else to do.

"Can I go now?" I ask.

"Give your ma a hug," she asks and she sits up on the sofa.

At first I don't want to but I can't say no to her and so we hug. I lay my head against her chest and she brushes my hair with her hand. Granny yells for her cups.

"You're a good boy, Michael," Ma says and lies back down on the sofa and goes straight to sleep.

twenty-two

Mr. McFadden and Miss Connor are having a Christmas wedding. She will wear a dress with a bit of fur over her shoulders given to her by my granny because as things turn out Granny also had a Christmas wedding. Miss Connor was pleased. She gave Granny a bunch of flowers and Granny nearly fainted she was so pleased. We had them in a vase in the middle of the kitchen table for everyone to smoke over. I didn't think it was fair to the lovely petals but no one cares, they want to smoke and so they will.

Everyone in the housing estate is going to be at this wedding. They are already buying dresses and shoes and bags, even though it is only October; even Marianne is excited and smiling again. She has been asked to sing in the church. She has chosen "Ave Maria" because that's what everyone sings at weddings. Dirty Alice is to read a passage about love, and Luke is to stand still and hold rings for the bride and groom.

"It will be very romantic," says Marianne.

"Yes, it will," says Dirty Alice, who has definitely changed her tune about Miss Connor, probably because of all the ice-cream money she's getting.

"Are you going to call her Ma?" I ask.

"Shut up," snips Dirty Alice, who wears braids now and all

kinds of things in her hair. I saw it wavy the other day, all the girls liked it and now they want the same for their stupid hair.

"Well, are you?" I ask.

"I'm to call her Louisa until I feel comfortable," says Dirty Alice.

"Not Stepmother?" I say and smirk a little. I'm trying to annoy her. I don't know why.

That's when Dirty Alice throws a clump of wet dirt into my face. It's heavy and it slaps right against my eye and I fall backward onto my arse. I want to kill her for it but my face is all muddy and I can't see a thing. Next thing she is on top of me and slapping the face off me and calling me all kinds of names. I don't know who pulls her off me but I can hear she is crying and that she hates me more than anyone in the entire world. I feel a bit wobbly on my feet and I want to get up and give her a good thumping but she's taken away by Luke. I see him look back at me. He doesn't look happy.

Marianne says, and not very nicely, "Alice gave you a right smack, didn't she?"

I don't say anything. I know she is trying to make me feel like I'm not tough anymore. A dangerous game to play considering what I know about her fanny. I could tell everyone.

"Alice backstabbed me. I didn't get a chance to defend myself. I was blinded by the dirt," I say.

Paul MacDonald and Fat Ralph agree. "It wasn't a fair fight. Alice is a girl and you can't hit girls back. She's dead lucky he didn't fight her 'cause he'd have kicked her arse into next week."

I nod and at the same time I'm pleased Paul and Fat Ralph have stood by me.

"Alice beat the crap out of him," says Tracey. "We all saw. Girls can fight as tough as boys."

"No, they can't," I say. All of a sudden I'm thinking of Ma being beaten by the rapist and I feel so bad I just want away from these stupid girls and their stupid words and their stupid faces.

"Who wants to go to the Woody?" says Fat Ralph.

The girls shake their heads. They always shake their heads when you talk about the Woody.

"What's the matter, you too scared?" says Paul, and then he laughs at them. "Come on, lads. Let's leave these tough ladies to tremble in their dirty little socks."

It was a funny thing to say and I laugh loudest, wishing I had said it. The girls are angry and want to say something clever back but they can't because girls aren't funny.

"If you think you're doing the talent show now, you're joking yourself," yells Marianne.

"Stick your talent show up your arse, Marianne," I say. "You'll never have one anyway and everybody knows it, you've been saying you'll have one for years and you never do. It's just an excuse so you can show off your stupid singing and dancing in the car park." Marianne starts to cry and the girls crowd round her, patting her on the shoulder. I don't care about Marianne Cameron anymore; her eyeballs can explode with tears for all I care. She's a dirty filthy girl. I wish I could tell the lads what she did, then they would think I was the best man in the entire Woody for seeing a girl's bits. But then Marianne might tell them how I ran away and I don't want any of the boys knowing I ran away from anyone's fanny. I would never live it down.

When we get to the Woody Paul and Fat Ralph want to look at nudie magazines but I don't feel like it and anyway Luke shows up with his hands on his hips like Granny does when she's about to get mad about something.

"Michael Murray, you come here right now," he says.

I know he's going to want to fight me and I really don't want to fight Luke because I would win and all the grown-ups would get mad at me for hurting the best boy in the entire world.

"You leave my sister alone, do you hear?" says Luke.

"She threw a clump of mud at my eye and then she jumped on top of me. She should leave *me* alone. She's a pain, your sister."

"You asked if she was going to call Louisa Ma. Did you not think that might have hurt her? She's at home now crying her heart out. Do you have no sensitivity? Our ma will always be our ma but we need to move on. Louisa is our friend. She is a good woman and is good to Alice and that's all that matters, not what we're going to call her when she's married to our father."

Luke has tears in his eyes because boys like Luke are allowed to cry and weep. If the grown-ups saw him all the women would crowd round him and tell him what a wonderful boy he is, and the boys who made him weep would be made to feel bad because he's too thin to beat up and too clever to argue with. Luke feels a lot older than the rest of us, like a little man, though there are only a few years between us all. One day we will have all caught up to each other in age and I wonder if I will still feel like Luke is too good for a hiding. The truth is, you can't be punching the likes of Luke, it's against some kind of law. It would be weak, a bit like Fat Ralph. You can get mad at Fat Ralph. You can push him about, give him Chinese burns and wedgies, but you can't fight him. It wouldn't be fair.

I wonder if I should say sorry to Dirty Alice, but since no one asks me to I decide not to bother. I'll just stay out of her way for a while. It's what Luke suggests anyway.

twenty-three

Halloween is my favorite time of year. I take a big goody bag and say "Trick or treat?" at every door I knock on. People like that round here, they don't want loud knocks and kids opening their bags expecting chocolates dumped into them before running off to the next house to do the same, especially Marianne's ma. She always asks for a trick and I always do my keepy-uppies. This means I always get good sweets and monkey nuts and toffee apples. Sometimes you get fruit. I hate fruit, but it's rude to complain. Once I got a toothbrush, that was the worst. One year people brought eggs to smack on people's windows who didn't like Halloween, like old folk with weak hearts and who maybe couldn't afford to buy the treats, so names were taken and arses were kicked. It never happened again.

I am a soldier this year and I have green all over my face. It's camouflage. Everyone thinks I look good. Paul is a farmer and sings "Old MacDonald" whenever he is asked for a trick, and Fat Ralph dresses like a girl. He says he is Marilyn Monroe and everyone laughs so hard they don't even ask him for a trick, which is a good thing because Fat Ralph can hardly do anything.

Marianne is a girl vampire and Dirty Alice is Charlie Chaplin. Fiona and Tracey go as Siamese twins all stuck together; they look funny like that and I like their costume the best.

Granny is giving out toffee apples and monkey nuts. Her toffee apples have a strange taste but no one cares on Halloween so long as they get something for their bags.

It is dark and cold out but you can't wear a jacket or you would ruin your look and so everyone freezes. The kids go in groups together and are not allowed to leave the housing estate; they have to stay in their own area. Ma makes a big fuss about this. The grown-ups are having their own party at the Bowling Club. Da isn't very original and goes as a vampire. Ma goes as a playing card, which is very unusual. She looks different from everyone and I think she is the best. She is the Queen of Hearts. My ma is clever to have made her costume. Granny helped her with the hearts though and makes a big fuss until Ma says, "I couldn't have done it without you, Shirley." This makes Granny feel better about missing the party and staying at home to give out her toffee apples and monkey nuts. Miss Connor and Mr. McFadden go as a nurse and a doctor. Everyone thinks this is hilarious, but you can't see Miss Connor's legs too well and her costume doesn't suit her at all. She is wearing thick white tights and a real nurse's uniform she borrowed from the infirmary up the road. She even has lace-up shoes and thick-rimmed glasses. She is white from head to toe except her lips, they're dark red, and so I suppose she is still the most beautiful woman in the world even if she is a boring nurse about to marry boring Mr. McFadden.

I am out for hours and when I get home I have the biggest bag of sweets you have ever seen in your whole life. I throw them onto the floor and separate the fruit from the pick 'n' mix, the chocolates from the dainties, and I make a big pile of monkey nuts, which are my favorite. I also make a pile of licorice and Spangles. I hate them. They make you shite too much. Granny has fallen asleep on the sofa and Ma and Da are out having a good time and so I can stay up late and no one will care. Then Paul MacDonald and Fat Ralph show up at the window and are tapping at it like a couple of eejits.

"What do you fools want?" I whisper.

"Michael," says Paul, "you have to come to the Woody."

"At this time of night? If I get caught outside this house past ten I'm a dead man," I say.

"Please, Michael. It's Miss Connor. She's been hurt," says Fat Ralph.

I put on my shoes and jacket all the time wondering what Miss Connor is doing in the Woody when she is supposed to be at the Bowling Club pretending to be a nurse.

Paul and Fat Ralph walk quickly. They're fairly rattled and explaining to me why they were in the Woody, like I'm a grown-up and I need to know.

"We were just looking for the nudie magazines, Michael, when we heard her. Someone's hurt her. It wasn't us."

When we get to the Woody it's pitch black but with strange noises, quiet noises, the kind the dark makes. Paul has a torch and flashes it in front of himself.

"She's over there."

Fat Ralph points to where Miss Connor is lying in a heap, a bundle of white. I hear her moaning.

"Gimme the torch," I say to Paul.

He hands it over.

"Come on," I say.

I don't want to go alone, I'm frightened, but they're more frightened and won't come with me. They've seen what I haven't and don't want to see it again.

"Michael," says Paul, "her clothes are ripped and she's naked in places. Can you give her your jacket? I'm not wearing one."

"I will," I tell him and take off my coat.

It's just a few steps to Miss Connor. She is lying on her side, her face swollen and bleeding, her clothes savaged by the same dog who savaged at my ma's clothes. I lay my jacket across her breasts. I know what I am looking at.

"Go get my granny," I scream.

Paul and Ralph don't move.

"Go get her!" I yell.

They start to run, leaving me alone in the Woody with Miss Connor. Her breath fades in and out and I think she might die. I want to stroke her hair and tell her it's OK, but I daren't lay a hand on her.

It's a few minutes before Granny comes rushing through the bushes screaming for Louisa. Granny gets to her knees and is crying for poor Miss Connor.

"Are the police coming, Granny?"

"They're coming, son," she says.

Soon the Woody is bursting with people. Miss Connor is deaf to it. They say she is half conscious. They have a mask on her to help her breathe and a pink blanket to keep her warm. I see the arm of my jacket falling from the side of the stretcher and think of her bleeding breast. I think of Marianne in the bushes and know there is a nakedness a boy is not supposed to see. It seems every neighbor we have is standing around the ambulance, blocking the police and all kinds of helpers. Miss Connor's stretcher slides into the ambulance driven by Kenny's da and when he sees Miss Connor's face he says, "Dear God." Luke goes with Miss Connor and holds her hand. Alice is to stay at Marianne's house until Mr. McFadden shows up. No one knows where he is and everyone is wondering if it was him that hurt her. I wonder the same. I wonder if Mr. McFadden hurt my ma too.

twenty-four

No one threw me from the kitchen, I just knew I wasn't supposed to be there and so I left the room and let them talk about poor Miss Connor and then listened at the door. Mr. McFadden had been with Ma and Da all night and so he couldn't have hurt Miss Connor.

Da said the party at the Bowling Club had been wild. Miss Connor had gotten drunk and was dancing with Patrick Thompson. Da said it made Mr. McFadden mad with jealousy and so he had a row with Miss Connor, who ran from the club in tears. Mr. McFadden stayed with Da and propped up the bar for the rest of the night.

"I couldn't get them away from the drink, Shirley," says Ma. "Oh God," she cries.

"They've arrested Patrick Thompson," whispers Granny. "They're saying Louisa went off with him on her own."

"Patrick Thompson?" says Da.

"Didn't he go with Tricia Law for a while?" says Granny.

"It can't be him. He doesn't smoke," says Ma.

"Then we have to go to the station and tell them that, Rosemary," whispers Da.

"If you go to that station I might get into some kind of trouble for not telling them about what happened to me," cries Ma.

No one had thought of that. I hadn't thought of that. If Ma had told the police she was attacked, then Suzanne wouldn't have been grabbed and Miss Connor wouldn't have been hurt.

"They'll hate me if I speak up now," says Ma, "I can't."

Ma was right. Everyone would hate her. Everyone would hate us, especially Louisa Connor, so would Mr. McFadden and Luke and Dirty Alice, but then she hates everyone so who cares about her. It was Miss Connor who would hate us the most. Her life was ruined because of Ma.

"Louisa will tell them the truth," says Granny, smoking. "Patrick has nothing to worry about. She'll tell them about the gold bracelet."

"What if Louisa doesn't know the truth? What if she didn't see a gold bracelet? What if he didn't smoke?" snaps Da.

"She's not going to say it was Patrick Thompson if it wasn't Patrick Thompson, is she?" shouts Granny.

"Let's hope not," says Da.

Everyone went to bed, but I don't think anyone slept at all. Ma was crying and Da was thirsty. I don't know if Granny slept but I bet she didn't. I know I didn't sleep a wink, but I must have, because when I opened my eyes it was morning already and I couldn't remember the dark at all.

twenty-five

Miss Connor identifies Patrick Thompson as the rapist and everyone believes her except Ma, Granny, and Da. I don't believe her either but only because I believe my ma, who says the attacker smoked in her face, and Patrick Thompson doesn't smoke at all. The attacker also wore a gold chain on his wrist like the one Suzanne Miller saw and since Miss Connor can't remember anything about the man who hurt her, the chain is not considered important enough, and because Ma won't tell about her attack or the gold chain, it just disappears from the evidence altogether. This is what Da has been saying all week, making Ma shout and cry.

Da is cut up about the whole thing. Patrick Thompson is the same age as my da. They drink in the pub together and sometimes they play darts. He doesn't live in the housing estate. He lives out by the shore in a tenement with his father, who is a very old man with gout, says Granny.

It's a quiet house again and when words are spoken they're spiky and sharp. I feel scared again.

When Miss Connor came home it was to Mr. McFadden's house and in a wheelchair pushed by Luke and Dirty Alice. Ma watched them from the window and even when they went into the house it was like she was rooted to the spot. She just stared at the door. Could have burned a hole through it.

Mr. McFadden and Miss Connor are still to be married but it will be a summer wedding now and Granny says the sooner the better because it is sinful of Miss Connor and Mr. McFadden to live together when they're not blessed by the Pope.

"What the fuck are you talking about? Louisa Connor has already been in hell and didn't we send her there ourselves?" screams Da.

Granny curls up at this and lights a fag.

Everyone has been very nice to Miss Connor since she came back, sending all kinds of lovely things to the house, but we didn't, not even a card.

The house is cold and Christmas is around the corner. I don't believe in Santa but I still want presents and I am worried Ma and Da have forgotten about me altogether.

I also worry for my new trousers. Every Christmastime I get a pair to match whatever jumper Granny or Ma has knitted for the school dance. When I remind Granny about the party she is delighted to produce the red-and-white jersey she knitted in the summertime. It's the most horrible thing you've ever seen, but it's also what I have to wear to the school dance and so I don't complain. Ma buys the trousers from McMillan's on the high street and they are too small for my legs. She never gets anything right. She's even stopped doing her course. It makes me angry and I want to scream at her for being so stupid for not noticing my size. I can actually see my ankles in the trousers she buys and so she takes them back to the shop, but there are no more in brown and so I have to wear a pair in girly cream. I hate them, but wear them anyway. I'm too fed up to care.

At the party I dance with lots of girls, but not Marianne or Dirty Alice. I would rather dance with Laura Jones, who lives on a farm and smells like a cow. I don't hold her hand though; I grab at her finger and twirl her around without touching her too much. She's a bit of a dog and it is embarrassing for any boy to be near her, but the teachers make you, otherwise she would sit in a corner and chew her own hands off.

When we sit down for our juice and our Christmas fairy cakes I start to feel sick. I can't explain it. My stomach starts to turn and I feel cold in my face.

"Are you all right, Michael?" says Mrs. Roy. "You're as white as a ghost."

"I'm fine," I say.

"Away to the nurse," she says.

"I don't want the nurse," I say.

"Come on now," says Mrs. Roy and takes me by the shoulder. "Let's go."

It embarrasses me to have the teacher lift me from my chair, everyone is looking, but I also feel unwell and think maybe I should go to the nurse.

When I stand up the room starts to wobble and I fall over and hit my head, that's how I end up in Kenny's da's ambulance. It is very clean.

When I get to the hospital, penlights are flashed across my eyes and pumps are placed upon my arms.

"He's fine," says the doctor to Ma.

"Thanks be to God," says Granny.

Da wasn't there. He was at home asleep no doubt, after his beers and his bottle.

"He just had a turn," says the doctor. "Keep a wee eye on him and if he has any kind of episode like today, then we'll send him up to Inverclyde and have him checked out properly."

Granny crosses herself.

Inverclyde is on the mainland and a very serious hospital; people go there when they have cancer or bad kidneys. When Grandpa Jake went to Inverclyde he never came back. I hope I never go to Inverclyde, and when they give me the orange juice to make me better I drink every last drop until I feel warm again.

"He's not eating enough," says Granny to Ma.

"He eats plenty," says Ma.

"You need some stew," says Granny. Ma rolls her eyes to heaven and I think maybe Inverclyde is a good idea after all.

twenty-six

Ma decides to do a spot of decorating before Christmas. She starts with the living room. It is a big job and we have to pull at the wallpaper with scrapers and knives to make the walls smooth and without crinkles.

"The new paper will look beautiful and without any creases or bumps," says Ma.

It is a boring job, scraping paper from walls, but everyone helps. Da goes mad about it all, especially when he has to move furniture and things like that. He moves it all anyway and then gets to the pasting. When the living room is done it looks nice and Ma decides the whole house has to be done. This isn't what Da wants.

"That's a big job, Rosemary," says Da.

"You can't have one room papered and the rest of the rooms looking like shit. If you're going to do a job, then let's do it," snaps Ma.

"I said no," whispers Da and then heads to the door.

Ma seems itchy. She has lots of energy all of a sudden and wants to do everything.

"What's the matter, Rosemary?" asks Granny.

"Nothing," she says, but it's something. She starts to tidy things away and this makes Granny annoyed because everything is already tidied away. Granny keeps the house spotless, but then Ma fetches a pail of water and starts in with the cleaning of the windows.

"I did them yesterday," nips Granny.

"I want to do them again," says Ma and that's what she does. She's rough with the cloth and the water and throws herself in and out of the pail like she wants to dive inside it and swim away. Granny leaves the room and lets Ma get on with it. I follow Granny. Ma is getting on all our nerves.

When Da comes back he brings home the biggest tree you have ever seen and it makes Ma as mad as a hare because it goes all the way to the ceiling and bends at the top. It's a brilliant tree, but Ma makes Da take it outside to cut the top off for the paper star. It is still too big and covers the front of the radiator and makes Granny think there will be a fire. I wonder the same but Da says everyone is daft. The tree even rips a little of Ma's new paper in the corner of the room and that makes Ma pull the worst face at Da's back. She is keeping her temper down, which isn't like her at all, but Da has a drink on him and so making faces at him when he can't see is the best thing to do. Granny keeps shaking her head at everyone but mostly the madness in Ma and Da.

"We have to buy more decorations for the tree, Brian," says Ma.

"What's wrong with the ones we have?" says Da.

"This is a bigger tree," says Ma. "We usually have a smaller one, our lights won't go once round this one. I don't have enough Christmas balls or tinsel either."

"Then we'll get them. You and me, Michael. What do you think? You'll need more chocolates no doubt if we're to cover the damn thing," says Da and this makes me excited. I always get chocolates spread across the tree wrapped in shiny paper and looking like wise men. It is good of Da to remind everyone. We'll need hundreds.

"It's late," says Ma.

"We have plenty of time," says Da.

Da eventually squeezes the tree into the corner of the room and it doesn't look bad at all, but Ma still hates it and walks from the room.

"I'll take Michael to the shops and get the decorations then. Come on, Michael."

I run for my socks and shoes but it's not a nice trip. We stop off at the pub first and Da has another pint. I am not allowed in the pub but I can have a lemonade and a packet of crisps on the pavement outside the bar. It's cold and my bum goes hard under my legs because Da takes a long time coming from the pub and I'm freezing. It's also getting dark and I worry Woolworths will be closing.

"Now don't be telling your ma or your granny about the pint, OK?"

I nod, although I am annoyed I have to lie about something so stupid.

"Let's go to Woolworths for those decorations now. If you're a good boy I'll get you an Advent calendar."

I'm sure the selling of Advent calendars is over, since Christmas Day is the very next day, but maybe if there are any left we might get a good deal on them. I'm hopeful anyway.

Da swings around Woolworths throwing everything and anything into the basket. I get my own basket for the chocolates. Da says I can have what I want and gets me two boxes of wise men. I am thrilled until I bump into Dirty Alice at the pick 'n' mix. Luke is at the records. I look around for Mr. Mc-Fadden and instead I see Miss Connor with her own basket; I don't know what she's buying. Anyway Da is on her aisle looking for shaving foam and when he sees the woman our family has shamed he jumps a little, but Miss Connor doesn't notice and seems glad to see him.

Watching them talk I can see Miss Connor has changed since the attack. She has long dark roots and she doesn't need the wheelchair anymore, although she walks with a limp on account of the damage done to her hip, that's what Granny says. Miss Connor and Da are in deep conversation when Mr. McFadden appears, carrying a hose. You can buy anything in Woolworths. Mr. McFadden and Da shake hands. Soon Da is nodding his head a lot, they are all talking very seriously, and suddenly Miss Connor's crying and in Mr. McFadden's arms. I wonder if Da has told them about Ma. That would be a disaster. Da pats Miss Connor's arm and she taps at his hand.

"Luke!" yells Mr. McFadden. "We're going."

Luke is paying for something at the record counter but when he sees how upset Miss Connor is he runs to her side like the good little boy he is. Everyone in the shop is staring at the drama.

"What did your stupid da say to Louisa?" snips Dirty Alice, who is not only picking the mixes, she is actually eating them without paying for them. What a little shoplifter. I hate her more than ever before.

When we get home Da doesn't mention Mr. McFadden or Miss Connor. He just gets busy around the tree. Granny has made mulled wine and I get hot Ribena. Da takes charge of the lights. It doesn't go well because the lights won't switch on and we have to spend a long time finding the faulty bulb and then replacing it with one that will make our tree be brilliant. We meddle for hours. Ma drinks all the mulled wine and then falls asleep on the sofa. Everyone forgets about the silver-wrapped wise men I have in my bag. I eat all of them.

The tree pops and Da is triumphant. It looks beautiful but Ma is asleep and can't see. Granny admires it but fusses around the branches across the radiator.

"I need to cut these away," says Granny.

"You'll do no such thing," snaps Da. "It's fine the way it is." Da leaves the room with a slammed door. Ma is jolted from her sleep.

"He'll have us burned in our beds," says Granny and pulls scissors from her apron, cutting all the branches that cover the radiator. It makes a C shape. Da will go bonkers, I think.

Despite the grumbling from Ma, she likes the tree but she is upset I ate the chocolates. We turn off the house lights and in the dark the tree sparkles and makes us all glad it is Christmas. It warms the room and for a minute everything feels good. I think of all the presents I will get. I think of the gloves I got for my granny, the comb I got for my da, and the chocolates with the pink bear that I got for my ma. Everyone will be pleased. We will eat turkey with roast potatoes, carrots, and brussels sprouts. I hate them but I will get them on my plate anyway. Granny will make her Christmas gravy and we'll have the pudding she ordered from the catalogue.

Da wants us all to go to chapel on Christmas Eve but Ma won't go.

"I have no interest in your icons and candles," says Ma.

"Then are you interested that Patrick Thompson is no longer a suspect in the Louisa Connor rape? Not enough evidence," says Da.

"Thank God," says Granny and crosses herself.

"I wouldn't look so relieved, Rosemary, because half this town still thinks he did it. Louisa Connor thinks she's being denied justice. She's beside herself with grief."

"At least he's not going to jail," says Ma.

"Jail would be a safer place for him right now. Everyone here hates him. And you do realize the real monster is still out there, that there might be more Louisa Connors, and then what? If anyone needs icons and the forgiveness of God, then it's you, Rosemary Murray."

"Then why don't you tell them?" Ma cries. "Go on, tell them. March into the police station and then come home to an empty house because I won't be in it anymore."

Da reddens with rage. He hates this truth. My ma is his one true weakness in life. He loves her more than his own breath. He would die if she left him. We all love Ma and she knows it. She climbs the stairs to her bedroom in silence. As she reaches the top Da shouts up after her.

"That's the stuff, Rosemary. You take one of your wee pills and this will all go away," shouts Da. Ma closes the door to her room and Da shakes his head in disgust.

"Are you coming, Michael?" Granny says, handing me my coat.

I nod and hope my ma won't hate me for going. I want to tell her that I am only going for her and that I will ask God to forgive her, that I will ask God to forgive us all.

twenty-seven

Even though it snows, Christmas Day is a disaster. I give out my presents and all I get are mumbles from Da, a kiss from Granny, and a pat on the head from Ma. There are no hugs or excitement from anyone except me.

I get a bike with streamers. It's a red Chopper. I could faint like a girl. I get an Etch A Sketch, a car that moves with batteries, an itchy pair of gloves, and a scarf knitted by Granny. I also get a Cadbury's stocking stuffed with chocolate, an Action Man with a truck, and a change of clothes. I am very happy with my loot, especially the chocolates in the stocking. You can never have enough chocolate on Christmas Day.

Da got Ma a coat. She said it was lovely.

"That's lovely, Brian," she says. "Thank you very much," and then she folds it onto the floor.

Da got Granny a blender, which she went mad for, and Ma got Da a shaver because Da has grown a beard and Ma hates it and so it was less of a present and more of a hint. Granny and Ma got each other the same thing because they cheated and went to Woolworths together. It was makeup and nail varnishes, even though Ma isn't making herself up too much these days. It was like no one could be bothered buying presents for each other, only me.

Dinner was quiet, we listened to Christmas songs on the radio, and I complained about the brussels sprouts; I always complain about the brussels sprouts. I don't know why anyone would grow them at all, they're rank. Anyway I wasn't very hungry with all the chocolate I had eaten but nobody cared too much. I still ate the pudding. I love the pudding.

I take my bike outside, mainly to show it off to the boys. I can't ride it on account of the thick snow but I want everyone to see it. Paul also got a bike, it's purple and it's a racer. I can see he's jealous of the Chopper though but he tries not to show it. Fat Ralph's ma and da have no money. His da is on the dole like mine, but he doesn't have a money pot like we have from Grandpa Jake and so Fat Ralph gets his ma and da's video re-corder for his bedroom, which is a bit of a shame, but it's also good news for us because we can watch pirate tapes and maybe we can get *E.T.* from Knobby Doyle. He also gets a stocking of chocolates and we're pleased for him. I tell him he can have first go of my Chopper when the snow lifts. He's pleased. We decide to have a snow fight and Dirty Alice, who got Sindy dolls and caravans and a doll's house for Christmas, comes to join in. I don't really want to play with her but it's snowing and you can't really stop people who want to throw snowballs at you. Anyway it's a good way to thump her and not get into trouble and so Dirty Alice gets my first snowball smack in the face, but Dirty Alice is fast and throws one right back at me and before you know it someone is shouting, "Snowball fight!" Everyone is at it except Marianne and Tracey, who make snow-men, then roll about making snow angels.

This is the best part of Christmas Day for me and I stay out until it is dark and with Dirty Alice of all people, but we get puffed out throwing snowballs and end up sitting in the snow together. No one goes to the Woody much these days, not since what happened to Miss Connor, and so we play on the hill instead.

"How is Miss Connor?" I ask.

"She's fine. They're getting married the weekend before Valentine's Day now, not the summer, did I tell you?" says Alice as if she should have told me because we're great big friends or something. Alice looks happy about the wedding and I feel sort of pleased for her.

"Are you sad for what happened to her, Alice?" I say.

She doesn't say anything for a minute. She knows what I am talking about and is wondering if she wants to discuss it with her arch-enemy.

"I'm sad the man that hurt her won't be punished, so is my da," says Dirty Alice.

She lies down in the snow and looks to the sky. I think she's going to make a snow angel but she doesn't. Dirty Alice would never make a snow angel. She just lies there and stares at the sky.

"It's very black, isn't it?" she says.

"What are you talking about? There's a ton of stars up there." I lie down next to her, thinking maybe I'll make a snow angel.

She turns to face me and says, "I'm not dirty, Michael. I know you say that about me but it's not true, and when you say it, it makes me hate you more than I do already, which is a big lot."

I am as red as can be. It's OK to call people names behind their back, but to be caught by the person and have them say something to you about it is a very embarrassing thing and so I try to think of something nice to say without being too sorry because it's Dirty Alice after all and I don't like her that much.

"You used to be dirty, all that tangled hair and the filthy clothes you used to wear," I say.

"Things are different now. We have Louisa to help us with the laundry and the house. Da is a new man because of her. That's what Luke says anyway. We love her," says Alice.

"I'm sorry," I say but not for calling Alice Dirty Alice, but for kind Miss Connor, who saved Alice's family and who was raped because of my family and our ugly secret.

Alice gets comfy in the snow and looks to the stars. She's wearing a purple jacket and a blue hat. Her mittens are red and her face is pink and I can see two little ponytails, one on each side of her head. She isn't even a little bit dirty. That's when I feel sorry for calling Alice names but I don't want to say sorry. I can't. She's still stupid, but for no reason at all I can't stop looking at her cheeks. They're so pink and warm and without even thinking about it I kiss her and Alice kisses me back, like a little poke on the face, and it feels strange and so we start throwing snow at each other until we are tumbling on top of one another. Alice is strong and pins me to the ground but I am stronger and roll around until she is pinned to the ground. I think she's going to beat me for sure now but she doesn't. She kisses me full on the mouth and not like Marianne, but in a nice way. She is gentle and I feel I could go at it for a long time. She tastes like Fizzy Lizzys. I don't even feel Mr. McFadden throwing me to the ground. It's all a big surprise.

"Da!" screams Alice.

Mr. McFadden is tearing at my jacket. I don't even see my

da pulling him away from me and then fighting Mr. McFadden. Everyone is crying around me. Miss Connor, Alice, and I think Luke. Granny is dragging me away and all because I kissed Alice McFadden, who is holding tight to Miss Connor and breaking her heart. I should never have kissed her. It was a bad idea. Alice is always getting me into trouble.

When we get home Granny says she is disappointed in me.

"You're too young to be messing with girls at your age," says Granny.

Da comes rushing in.

"Are you all right, son?" says Da while at the same time squeezing his face in rage when he sees my torn jacket. "I should kill the bastard for this," says Da and goes for his coat.

"You already had a go," says Granny. "Enough is enough. What the hell do you think you were doing, Michael?"

I am too ashamed to say "kissing" and so I shrug my shoulders.

Ma, who never went outside and just watched from the window, says, "You only kiss girls who want to be kissed. You're NOT to be rolling them onto the dirt and making them." She bangs the table with her fists.

"That's not what happened," I cry. "Alice and me were playing a game. She wanted me to kiss her."

"For God's sake. He's your son, Rosemary, and he was kissing his sweetheart and you think . . . what do you think, Rosemary?" asks Da.

"Alice and me were just fooling about, Ma. There was nothing in it, really."

"Shame on you," says Da to Ma.

Ma has thought something bad about me and then she thinks something bad about herself.

"Oh, Brian," she cries.

Da goes to Ma's side and takes her hands. They just sit there holding hands. Ma feels sorry, I can see it in her face.

Granny and I go to the sitting room and sit on the sofa. Granny looks tired. She has her arm around me.

"I meant what I said, Michael, you're too young to be kissing girls," she says. "But if you find you can't stop yourself, then you need to talk to your father, understand?"

I nod, but I have no idea what she is talking about.

twenty-eight

Patrick Thompson is in intensive care.

"They kicked the shit out of him. He's in Inverclyde now, a broken breastplate," says Da.

Ma grabs for Frankie's lead. Frankie gets all excited, just the noise of the lead makes Frankie mental. He loves to go for walks.

"Taking the dog out," Ma says.

Granny and Da exchange looks. Ma clips the door behind her. I finish my toast. I think of going with her but I want to hear more about Patrick Thompson.

"No one saw a thing," says Da to Granny.

Granny shakes her head and crosses herself.

It's a terrible thing to keep crossing yourself, I think. It's like forgiving yourself every minute of the day for things you can't really forgive yourself for, as if you're saying that you're still a good person even though you know you're telling lies and keeping secrets you shouldn't.

Da doesn't cross himself; he lowers his eyes to his paper and gives it a shuffle. There is nothing we can do for Patrick Thompson but there is something we could have done and didn't.

Everyone knows Ma would leave us if we didn't keep this

lie for her. We have seen her packed suitcase before and it frightened the life out of us all. We couldn't be without Ma. We would be lost without her. Da would be lost without her. We love Ma.

I think of Alice all the time and the kiss in the snow, and then I think of her da tearing at my jacket, but he's very sorry about that and Mr. McFadden comes to the door with a leather soccer ball for me. He is actually weeping. Granny has to give him a cup of tea. Ma hides upstairs. She can't face Mr. McFadden or Louisa Connor or anything to do with their family. Mr. McFadden tells Da and Granny the last few months have been hard on the family and when he saw me with Alice something inside him snapped.

"They're too young to be kissing," says Mr. McFadden.

"It's a scandal is what it is," says Granny. "Too much TV."

Da doesn't say anything, he just bites his lip, because when he first kissed Ma she was only twelve and he was fourteen. They have loved each other that long.

Every day I feel like a big horrible liar and it's been like that for a long time now. Whenever I see Miss Connor waving through her window or Luke or Alice I feel sick in my stomach. My hands go sweaty and I feel like I might have a heart attack or something. I don't even care about my keepy-uppies anymore, although it was nice of Mr. McFadden to get me the cool new ball. It is so hard to concentrate on anything these days and I dread the talent show. Marianne announces it will be on New Year's Eve and everyone thinks this is a brilliant idea except me because I know I will be rubbish and it will be freezing outside.

Ma says it will be fun to go to the talent show and seeing

Ma cheered about it makes me think there might be something wrong with her. I don't think she understands she will have to talk to Miss Connor at the concert and say Happy New Year to her and do the same to Mr. McFadden, who might kiss her on the cheek. She might also have to clap for Alice when she sings her songs and have to be shocked and surprised when Luke the Magician does his amazing trickery. At the moment she hides from them all, but she can't hide at the talent show. She will have eyes to look through and words to find. Right now she has none and so I dread the talent show and I wonder if my ma's mind will get sick again. I hope Da never leaves her side.

With all the sadness that's been in the housing estate Skinny Rab decides we will also have fireworks and sausages in buttery rolls. It is a great excitement and Marianne can hardly breathe for the joy of it. Her da is her da again. On New Year's Eve her ma makes sausages and passes them around and everyone eats them and laughs and acts like Tricia Law never existed at all.

Marianne has gathered everyone around her for the talent show, even me, who was banned from having anything to do with it. No one reminds her, not even Alice, who hasn't looked at me since I kissed her in the snow, though I did see flaky sneak peeks every now and then. I wonder if she would like to kiss me again.

The talent show costs five pence and all proceeds will be given to the Salvation Army instead of the kids because the grown-ups thought it was a better idea. I think it is a rubbish idea. Anyway, the Salvation Army agrees to come to our show and give a little service and play God songs with their brass band. This annoys Granny, who thinks the Salvation Army is not a real religion and the priest should be asked to give a service instead. Marianne's ma agrees with Granny but for the sake of the kids they say nothing and pay their five pence.

Luckily the Salvation Army don't give a service, they just turn up and say "Hello" and "Thank you" and go straight to playing their music. Everyone is glad. They play "Amazing Grace," something that makes Granny cry, and then "Auld Lang Syne," which is fun because we all hold our hands together and make a kind of wave. Then they collect the five pences for the show and take a seat like everyone else.

It's a big turnout. People bring their own chairs to sit on and blankets to keep themselves warm. The streetlights shine up the pretend stage, which is really a concrete car park, and Marianne begins with "Ave Maria." She makes all the old ladies weep. Then she does the Highland fling with Tracey, Fiona, and Alice. There is a lot of clapping going on and when they finish everyone stands up and claps some more, which is no surprise. Marianne is an award-winning dancer and was always going to amaze everyone. Marianne sings more songs and you would think it was "The Marianne Show," but she does sing a song with Alice and it's quite nice, Alice has a lovely voice too, but then there is more dancing and it gets a bit boring. Fiona and Traccy hardly do anything except dress up as Japanese girls and sing about a boy they really love. Luke does a magic show and it is quite good, he uses cups and things and tries to trick the grown-ups with pebbles and eggs; mostly I'm glad he didn't play chess because that would have bored me to death. Sarah from Robertson Drive does jokes that aren't funny but everyone rolls about the floor. Christian from Eaglesham Road plays "Twinkle, Twinkle, Little Star" on a trumpet and the audience raves, even though he is off tune. I hate this trumpet talent. Paul and Fat Ralph dress up as women and dance about like a couple of fools. I am embarrassed for them, but the adults love it. Then Auld Ian from the top terrace, who is about a thousand years old and not supposed to be in a kids' talent show, recites a Robert Burns poem about a red rose and again all the women cry all over the place.

When it is my turn I am nervous and shaking a little, but I know I am the best at keepy-uppies and will have the greatest talent in the show. But the first time I put the ball on my knee it falls to the ground. I look to my da and he gives me the thumbs up. I try again, but I only manage two. It is pure humiliation. Marianne and Paul snigger and Alice and Fat Ralph look sad for me. I look to Ma and see her picking at her nails. She is doing anything she can to stop from looking up, from seeing faces, from seeing Miss Connor. She doesn't even care it's my turn. I don't know why she is there at all. Anyway I get to twenty and everyone shouts and whoops like I did a hundred or something when I haven't. I am gutted. I know I have done rubbish and so I don't know why they are clapping at all. I look around then and see men and women with beer cans and wine bottles in their hands and that's when I realize everyone is drunk or most people. I see Miss Connor smiling and waving at me with a huge smile when the truth is she probably hates to smile. Next to her Mr. McFadden is tipping beer into his mouth and cheering with a sausage roll in his hand when it was only a week before he tore at my jacket for kissing his daughter. They're faking it. Everyone is pretending they like our talents when the truth is they just want to get drunk for New Year's and probably think we're all shite. Fuck them all, I think.

"Are you all right there, Rosemary?" says Miss Connor,

who positions herself right in front of Ma. Ma never saw it coming and takes a bit of a while before saying, "I'm good, Louisa."

"Haven't seen you in a while. You look well," says Miss Connor.

"So do you," says Ma.

"Weren't the kids wonderful?" says Miss Connor.

Ma goes blank and says nothing for a minute. I think of interrupting and filling in the gap, but then Ma says, "I'm sorry, Louisa, I need the bathroom. Was nice to see you."

Ma rushes to the bathroom, even though I know she doesn't need to go at all and is running from Miss Connor.

"Is everything all right?" whispers Miss Connor to me.

I shrug my shoulders and run to where Da is. He is helping light up the fireworks until they start to whistle and hit the sky. Faces light up and everyone raises their tins and bottles to the stars. All the kids are given sparklers and told to be careful. I love the sparklers, I can't help it, they make me feel happier, and so I decide to tell my own lies. I tell Marianne she will be on *Top of the Pops* one day. I tell Paul and Ralph they were hilarious in lipstick and I ask Luke to show me his magic tricks, even though it's hard to follow. I don't tell Alice anything. I will not lie to Alice, even though she tells me I am the best at keepy-uppies in the world.

Lies make people happy, I think, and that's why people tell them, not to hurt or anger anyone, but to keep them safe from the truth, except our lie, the lie Ma and Da and Granny are telling to themselves and everyone else around them, it is the worst of lies and it is making no one happy and when lies don't make you happy you have to wonder what will happen next.

twenty-nine

I t's my birthday and I am twelve. I was born four days after New Year's Eve and during the Christmas holidays. It's a shite time to have a birthday because no one has any money left from all the Christmas presents they bought you, but it's better than having Paul's birthday; he was born on Christmas Eve and gets even less than I do. We are always complaining of it.

Da asks if I would like to have a few friends round for my birthday, but I say no. I hate my house right now. Da smells of beer and Ma is always cleaning things. She is driving Granny mad with it.

Ma starts her studies again in a few weeks and Granny is relieved Ma will have something to do other than windows Granny has already cleaned and rooms that never needed decorating in the first place. Ma has papered Granny's room and her own. She also papered the hallway a weird brown color. I wouldn't let her touch my room and I made the biggest fuss a boy could make over it. She is like a train right now but a train that stays indoors. She is terrified of bumping into Miss Connor. We are all glad she is starting her studies again. She is a pest in the house.

"It will certainly occupy her. I can't stand all this running around she's doing," moans Granny.

If Ma does well she can go to Jordan Hill and be the teacher she always dreamed she would be. Da thinks this is great, but he says this about everything Ma wants. It's annoying, but she likes it, it soothes her.

"I'll make a nice cake for your birthday," says Granny.

"I don't want people here for a party."

"Then what do you want for your birthday?" asks Ma.

I shrug my shoulders because I really don't know.

"How about a portable television for your room?" says Da and gives me a wink.

I jump for joy. There is nothing I would like more.

"A television!" nips Ma. "Are you mad?"

"He's old enough and what with you hogging ours all the time for your learning he could do with his own TV," says Da.

"He'll be up all night," says Ma.

"I won't. I promise," I say.

"Now look what you've done," says Ma. "How can I say no now when you've already said that he can!"

"What's the big bloody deal?" says Da. "It's a television not a fucking atomic bomb."

Granny slams the iron down onto the board.

"That's enough, the two of you. Rosemary, let the lad have his TV for God's sake, and Brian, you should have discussed this with your wife first. That wasn't fair of you."

The room is silenced. Ma grabs for Frankie's lead and I am getting a TV.

I run out the back door to tell the lads but there's no one

there except Alice and so I run back inside and hide till she's gone. She takes a long time to leave. I don't know where she went, probably to stupid Marianne's house.

I go to the Woody to see if the lads are there but there's no one except Ma. I don't know what she's doing but she's standing where Miss Connor was found. She doesn't see me but Frankie does and I think he's going to give me away with his tail wagging about the place, but Ma doesn't even look up. She is stuck in space. Staring at the grass. Frozen like a statue. I sneak from the Woody; seems I'm hiding from everyone these days. I go home.

"What are you doing here?" says Granny.

"Nothing," I say.

"Nothing?" says Granny and then pulls a face, as if she doesn't believe me. Grown-ups hate it when you say "nothing." They really have a problem with it. I use it all the time and for everything I have no answer to, but they make this big thing out of it as if you're hiding the Crown jewels in your schoolbag.

When Ma gets back she goes over to Da and gives him a hug and the whole house stills.

"A TV is fine," Ma whispers, and so Da and Ma go buy me a TV.

The TV is white and a good size. It is also a color TV so it must have cost Da an arm and a leg. Granny gives me money for my birthday. A whole five pounds. They tell me to save it. I feel like a millionaire. I will buy a hundred things with it.

I am so excited I decide to go to Paul's house and see if he wants to come out, but mostly so I can tell him about my television. Paul is pleased for me and comes up with the great idea of using Fat Ralph's video recorder to watch some of Knobby Doyle's pirate videotapes and so that is what I decide to do on my birthday, watch *Raiders of the Lost Ark* in my room with my pals. Fat Ralph thinks this is a brilliant idea. I tell my da and he agrees to get the pirate tape.

Granny doesn't have time to make a cake. She buys one from the baker's. It is an amazing cake, green with white icing and my name written across the top. I know I am about to have a great birthday, but then I see Alice sitting on the step outside her house playing with stones and I feel bad for her, but I also don't want her near me, but I can't leave her sitting on her own while I eat cake and so I ask her in. Paul and Fat Ralph think I am mad. Alice quickly asks her da. She doesn't want to play stones on her own. Her da says yes and Alice comes into my house. It's a big thing her da says yes and Da gives him the thumbs-up.

"I'll watch them, don't worry," Da says.

Mr. McFadden gives Da the thumbs-up.

Everything is OK and everyone is happy on my birthday.

We all go to my room and I am pleased to see Ma has tidied it for my friends. Da sets the TV and video recorder up for us to watch the movie and Granny brings the food: paste sandwiches, jelly and ice cream and the beautiful green cake.

The movie is the best movie in the world but Alice hides behind cushions in parts because it is also a scary movie. This is what all girls do. It is what Ma does, she hides behind her hands but still watches through her fingers, which is stupid because it just means she's watching a film with her fingers in the way. To be honest, there are bits of the film where I want to hide behind a cushion, but I don't. I am the toughest lad in the housing estate and it would be terrible of me to grab at my pillow and hide like a girl and so I squeeze my eyes at the frightening bits so they are a little bit hidden. Fat Ralph doesn't care and grabs at the skirt of my bed, but it's OK for Fat Ralph to be scared because he's Fat Ralph. Paul, on the other hand, is scared of nothing and laughs at the scary bits and then watches everyone else to make sure they are as brave as he is.

When the film is finished we have cake and lemonade, then Paul gives me a pack of soccer cards, which was very nice of him, and Fat Ralph gives me his Celtic pencil. They're not real birthday presents, everyone was invited at the last minute, but they're nice all the same. Alice is shy because she didn't have anything for me, but since her da got me a leather soccer ball for kissing her I let her off.

The cake is nearly finished when Paul spills lemonade all over the floor. I think my ma might kill me and so I go to the landing and into the airing cupboard where we keep the towels and the blankets for guests, even though we never have guests. I have to dig hard for towels because they are stuck right at the back and that is when I find a plastic bag. I pull it out, thinking maybe it is a surprise gift for me, but it isn't. It is a bag of dirty clothes: a dirty jacket, and a ripped shirt with what I think might be blood. There is also a filthy skirt and it is dry with mud. It doesn't take me long. I know exactly what I am holding in my hands. It is what my ma was wearing the night she was attacked. I don't know what it is doing hidden in the airing cupboard. I don't know why she kept such horrible things. Why they are still dirty and why they are not in the bin with the eggshells and banana peels. It makes me feel sick. I am holding rape.

"What's taking you so long?" says Alice from behind me. She sees the bag.

"What's that?" she says.

"Laundry," I say and I shove it back where I found it.

"Looks dirty," she says.

"It's Da's. He wears it in the garden," I say.

She turns on her heels and goes back to her cake and lemonade. I go back to my party.

"Where's the towel?" says Paul.

I forgot and go back to the airing cupboard. I can still see the white of the bag and push it as hard as I can out of view. I grab for a towel and go back to Paul and his clumsy drink.

I want the party to be over now and when Alice's da comes to the door to collect her I am relieved. It is already dark outside and everyone leaves my bedroom with their dirty dishes lying all over the floor and across my bed. Ma nips in later and picks up plates and glasses. I go to help her but I can't keep myself from staring at her. That's when Da appears and says, "The birthday boy is free of all chores for today. I'll help you, Rosemary."

I see her smile at Da. She is in a good mood with him today and I wonder if Da knows about the clothes in the airing cupboard. Ma is mad, I think. I wonder if anyone else in the house thinks the same.

"You've lost a lot of weight, Rosemary," says Granny at dinner.

"Don't have much of an appetite, Shirley," says Ma.

"And for a long time now," says Granny.

"I wouldn't worry about it. You know what they say. You can never be too rich or too thin."

Granny looks at Ma for a sharp second and then to her own plate and I think Granny thinks the same as I do. Ma is not as well as everyone likes to think.

I don't know what to do with the clothes in the airing cupboard and wonder if I should tell my da. I don't want to keep any more secrets and so I bother him watching TV. He doesn't like that one little bit, but what else can I do?

"What do you want?" he asks.

I don't want Ma to know what I have found and I definitely don't want Granny to know. She's already worried about Ma's weight. I speak in whispers, but Da's a bit deaf sometimes and screws his face up and gets on my nerves.

"Would you come to the landing so I can show you something?" I tell him.

"What is it you want to show me?" asks Da, who is kind of ignoring me as if I'm not very important and have nothing to say really.

"Come on, Da, Ma might come." I tug on his sleeve.

"For the love of God, Michael, I just want to watch TV in peace. Away upstairs and play with your Action Men or something," nips Da.

"Please, Da," I beg. "Before Ma comes," I say.

Da looks at my face and knows there is something serious going on with me and even though he sighs and complains he follows me up the stairs anyway.

When I show Da what Ma's been hiding he goes as white as a ghost.

"Why is she keeping these things, Da? Should we put them in the bin?" I say.

Da looks very serious at me. "No," he says and pushes the

bag to the back of the cupboard. "Your ma knows why she's keeping them. We don't have to," says Da. "Pretend you never saw them, son," he tells me.

And that's what I do. I've told my da and I've shared a secret. It feels good. I wish I could share all my secrets, but I can't. I have to keep all the stories and all the words locked inside my head but I wonder for how long.

thirty

Miss Connor is having a baby and Mr. McFadden is delighted. He told my da first because he fancies they are great friends, even though he gave me a beating at Christmas time. Granny crosses herself at the mere mention of Miss Connor's baby.

"She's almost four months now. They thought she might lose it after what happened but it's a strong wee thing and wants to be here. It's a miracle for them. You believe in miracles, Rosemary? On getting on with things?" says Da and with a right nasty tone on him. He is drunk.

I think Ma will cry at this, but she grabs for the dog's lead and practically runs out the front door while Da reaches for the bottle next to the sugar, but Granny takes it away from him and I can hear her shouting.

"It's little wonder you sleep on a sofa with the smell of drink on you. Look at the state of you. I wouldn't touch you with a shitty stick."

"What difference does it make? Rosemary isn't interested in me. Haven't you heard all of this is my fault?" says Da.

"You want your wife to take an interest in you, then take an interest in yourself," says Granny.

Granny isn't one for leaving rooms with a slammed door

behind her. She likes to make people feel uncomfortable and so she heads to the stove to cook something we'll have to eat later.

Ma gets back in time for tea and she is smiling. Walking Frankie always brings out the best in her. Da has had a bath and is wearing a nice jersey. He looks good but he still has a big belly.

"The wedding's been moved forward to the weekend before Valentine's Day. What do you think of that?" says Da.

"Romantic," says Ma.

"The sooner the better. Living together but unmarried and with a baby on the way. It's a disgrace," says Granny.

"She's converting, you know," says Da.

"She is?" Granny is all impressed.

"She is," says Da. "Wants to be a Catholic and marry in the church."

"Then God will be kind to her and we'll say no more about it," says Granny.

Ma is quiet all through dinner. Da too. He drinks milk like me. No beer.

Granny tries to break the silence by talking to Frankie and giving him some gristle. Da pets him and so does Ma. He sits between them.

"Away you go, you daft dog," giggles Ma.

"He's daft all right."

"Can I go upstairs to my room and watch a bit of TV, Ma?" I ask.

"Did you finish your vegetables?" Da asks.

I nod.

"OK, but not too much or your eyes will go square," says Granny.

I go upstairs and turn on my television but there is nothing on and so I open my window and see if there's anything to watch. That's when I see Ma and Da admiring Da's efforts in the garden. Ma complains of being cold and Da puts his arm around her. His arm is like a stone arc and he barely touches her shoulder. When she brings his arm in closer I feel funny. I don't know what I'm looking at. Granny puts the radio on and brings out a couple of mugs of tea into the garden for them before leaving Ma and Da alone to admire the snowdrops. It's so dark and so cold outside I wonder how long Ma and Da will last, but the tea is doing its job and is keeping their hands warm. Da says something funny and Ma laughs. They are completely alone and I feel bad for spying on them but I can't help it. They are my ma and my da. They belong to me. I want them to dance in the moonlight or something but I know that won't happen. It makes me want to cry. They will stand around with mugs of tea and care about white and yellow flowers when I want my da to take my ma in his arms and waltz her around the garden, but it's not how they love. I wonder if they have ever danced.

I go to bed watching TV. I'm not supposed to watch TV in bed, but since everyone is busy in the garden loving flowers in the dark no one cares what I am doing. I pretend to be asleep when Da comes into my room to turn off my television and when he leaves I expect him to go downstairs. I hear him on the landing outside his own bedroom door. I wait for the door to open but it doesn't and so I hear my da climb back down the stairs to the sofa, but then the door is suddenly opened by Ma.

"Brian, where are you going?" she says.

No one says anything for a moment and I am perfectly

still. Da walks back up the stairs to Ma. I hear their bedroom door close shut, but then Frankie comes behind them and is scratching to be let in. I think he is going to spoil everything. Ma opens the door and whispers, "Just for tonight, Brian. He's a poor wee thing."

"Let the daft dog in then," says Da, but he's not angry.

I hear Frankie take a run to their bed. I hear shoes kicked off and a mumbling of talk.

I switch the TV back on and keep the volume low and watch a movie about Dracula. There are stakes and all kinds of mad things. I watch it through my fingers like Ma does. It's the best movie I have ever seen. I don't remember falling asleep but when I wake up someone has turned off my television. I don't know who.

thirty-one

O ur official wedding invitation arrives from the McFaddens and it is decided we can't go. We still feel the shame about what we did to Miss Connor. We will send a gift and make our excuses. We will go to Glasgow for the day but say we are visiting a sick relative instead. We will not say we are going to see *E.T.* and have a bite to eat. Da says we will visit the big bookshop for Ma and maybe we will go to the Barrowland, where you can buy anything in the whole wide world. It's the biggest flea market in the universe, Da says. Granny wants to buy wool but Da says we are not to shop too much because if we are caught going back on the boat with bags from Poundstretcher and from What Every Woman Wants, then everyone will know we didn't go to the wedding on purpose and went on a shopping spree on the mainland instead.

When Da tells Mr. McFadden he can't be an usher at the wedding Mr. McFadden thinks it is because of what happened at Christmas time between Alice and me. Da makes up a great story about Granny's brother being very sick with no family to care for him and because of the nice present from Ma and Da, a coffee maker that tells the time, the McFaddens are fooled and we can go about the business of lying to them again.

Their wedding is on a Saturday before the romantic day of Valentine's and is in the chapel. She will be a beautiful white bride with a fur collar, the one Granny gave to her. Granny weeps at the thought of it and makes Louisa promise to show her photos, which makes Ma go crazy. She doesn't want Miss Connor's image anywhere near the house. Ma is afraid of Miss Connor. I hate her for that because Miss Connor never did any harm to Ma, it was the other way around.

It will be a great wedding and I am sorry to be missing it. Mr. McFadden will throw a shower of pennies to the children waiting outside the church and then everyone will go to the Glenland Hotel for a big party. Alice and Marianne will be gorgeous bridesmaids but then Alice will spill something on her lovely dress, because she is Alice and that is what she does. Luke will wander around and talk with grown-ups with his arms behind his back and they'll nod at him as if he is also a grown-up or maybe even a teacher. He is very full of himself, that Luke, but everyone loves him and he can be anything he wants. Fat Ralph and Paul will eat all the cake and drink so much apple juice they'll pee their pants. I really want to go to this wedding and pee my pants but I know I can't.

Every day I pray the truth will come out and last night I wrote a letter.

Dear Miss Connor,

I am sorry for what the man in the Woody did to you. My ma was in the park and he did the same to her but she would not tell a soul because she was frightened to death of what the people in town would think of her and then he did it to you and she feels very bad and we all feel very bad and we are sorry you feel the baddest. We hope you have a nice wedding and a beautiful baby.

From Michael Murray

PS Please don't hate us, because he is a pervert who has hurt us all and we should get him.

I thought of Ma reading that letter and I felt bad again. I ripped it up straightaway. I even thought of eating it in case she found it and put the pieces together. And so I went to the Woody and set it alight. It was a tiny burning and no flames caught the grass because it was damp and so there was no big fire and I didn't die. The letter is gone now but I still have the postage stamp and I will send Alice a Valentine's card instead or it will be a terrible waste.

Ma is the final word around here and there is to be no wedding and no McFaddens spooking around our lives, making her feel awful about herself and all the things that have happened to her, but the McFaddens live behind us and it is hard not to wave at them and smile and ask Mr. McFadden how his back is or even watch his beautiful future wife walking to the shops in her satin trousers or even send a Valentine's card to Alice, but I will send one anyway because it is a secret card and I will not write anything inside so she can't tell my writing and will never know who sent it to her anyway. No one will.

What I really want is for Ma to tell people what happened to her, to tell Miss Connor what happened to her and to stop running away from her like a big frightened baby because that is what she is. Even her tea is frightened; every time Ma picks a cup up she shakes like a jelly. I feel scared she can be like this and I have to get my own tea these days for fear she would see me watching her wiggling all over the place.

I have so many questions. I want to know why she keeps her clothes from the night of the attack in a plastic bag in the airing cupboard. I want to know why she visits the spot where Miss Connor was raped whenever she takes Frankie for a walk. I want to know why she hasn't got Da to go looking for a rapist with a gold bracelet.

Ma is a very strange person to me. I want to love her like I used to, I really do, but she doesn't love me like she used to and so she gets what she gets. I am a different boy now.

thirty-two

On the day of the wedding we are on the six-thirty boat. We don't want to see anything at all, not a limousine or a flower, not a bottle of champagne, or even Miss Connor in rollers looking out of her window or Mr. McFadden fetching the milk so they can all have a relaxing cup of tea before going to the chapel. We are different from other people because we want their big day to be over and want to be back in our house while they are all at the hotel singing and dancing and having a good old time.

But the trip to Glasgow is the worst day of my life. Ma wouldn't come to see *E.T.* and so it was just Da and me. It was a great movie and I didn't cry at all. Da nearly cried; I think I saw a teardrop. He gets sad easy, my da. I was happy for E.T. He got to go home with his ma. Elliott would just have to find himself another friend.

Granny wanted some new patterns and some wool to knit me a sleeping bag or something mad like that and Da was sad Ma wouldn't come see the movie with him. She said she wanted to check out the bookshop, which had a million books in it, and so I said I would go later and maybe get myself a book and Da thought that was a good idea. We had great fun watching the movie. I had popcorn and sausages and big cups full of Coca-Cola. I stuffed my face and had to go to the bathroom afterward for a big shite. That was Granny's fault for making me eat porridge before we left.

There is a bar behind the cinema and Da asks if he can have a quick one while I wait outside. This annoys me. He's been so good lately but since Ma and Granny are not around I see no shame in it. He goes in and as usual brings me out a packet of crisps and a glass of lemonade. I am in no mood for crisps or lemonade after the shite I've just done but I take them anyway, no point in wasting them. It's not a warm day and I get colder than I would like but Da is as good as his word and quickly leaves the pub after one pint and so we make our way to the Barrowland.

It's a busy place all right. It's like there are thousands of people there. They're selling fish and cakes, flowers and newspapers. Sausages in rolls and chicken on skewers. I see someone selling Virgin Mary dolls and all kinds of religious toys. Granny is mad for it and buys two Virgin Marys and a Jesus Christ doll. There are clothes everywhere you look and music blares from all corners. Then there are doors opening up to dark rooms where people buy things they're not supposed to.

"Like what?" I ask Da.

"Pirate videos, son."

"What Knobby Doyle sells?"

Da nods. "A person has to make money somehow. Margaret Thatcher's seen to that."

I am glad Da is talking about Margaret Thatcher again. I am glad he is sleeping in his own bed again with Frankie and

Ma, although I wish he hadn't had a pint. Ma will smell it on him and be angry with the both of us.

Ma is not at the Barrowland. We are supposed to meet her at the fish stand at five, but then we move from the fish stand and because we move we think we might have missed her.

"We should have stayed where we were," moans Granny.

It gets darker and so we decide to go back to the bookshop and that's where we find Ma huddled in a corner with a man about six foot with a head full of dark gray hair. He looks older than Da, but not much older, and he is sitting very close to my ma. They have a book between them. When Ma sees Da she reddens. The man turns to see what Ma is looking at. He sees Da and gives him a big friendly smile, but Da does not smile, Da has another face on him altogether.

"Brian, this is my professor, Terrence Bodwin," says Ma.

This man does not look like he's ready for retirement any day soon and Granny looks nervous. Da says nothing, but looks like he's going to say something and something not very nice.

"Pleased to meet you, Professor Bodwin," says Granny.

The friendly professor gives Da his hand, but Da won't take it. It's very embarrassing. He just keeps staring at it and it feels like a bomb is going to go off. The professor withdraws his hand.

"I've heard so much about you all," says the friendly professor. "Rosemary is a star student. She'll go far."

"Will she now?" says Da.

"One hundred percent," says the friendly professor. "With the right support."

"What kind of support?" says Da.

"Brian, give it a rest," says Ma.

"I should go, Rosemary," says the friendly professor.

Ma nods but her face is so red. The friendly professor "bids" us farewell and moves on. He gives Da a funny look as he walks by us and then a big handsome smile to my granny, who almost faints at his good looks.

Ma picks up her bag and her shopping. She folds the book she was poring over with her friendly professor into her bag, but really roughly, like she could shove it right through the bag. She's fuming.

"What was he doing here?" asks Da.

"I bumped into him. Jesus, you were rude."

"Ready for retirement, you said," nips Da.

"What does it matter how old he is?" snaps Ma.

"Why did you tell him, a man like that? Did you want to get his attention, Rosemary? Is that it? Did you want him to feel sorry for you? Maybe like you more?"

"For what? Being RAPED?" she screams.

The entire store looks up at us. I can hardly breathe. Ma said "raped" in a bookshop. Someone else says, "Shhhh," and Da says, "Fuck off."

Ma runs away.

"Go after her, Brian," says Granny.

"No. I'm done," says Da and when we get on the train it's without Ma.

"This isn't right, Da," I say.

"She's a big girl, your ma. She'll find her own way home," says Da.

Granny takes my hand. I let her but I am scared of leaving Ma behind and I am scared my da is letting her be left.

I let go of Granny's hand and jump from the train. The doors slide over and the train moves on. Da is beating on the glass doors, but it's too late. I run off to find my ma. I will not leave her behind.

thirty-three

I run into the terminal and scan the station for my ma. I think I see her at a shop that only sells socks. It's not her. My ma is taller than this woman and is wearing a green woolen hat. I hear whistles and trains. It's a noisy terminal but I'm not frightened and I am glad I let go of my granny's hand. I am twelve now and there's no need for a boy like me to be scared of anything. I will find Ma and we can go home together.

For a moment I think she might be at the bookshop and I should go straight there, but then I remember she said "raped" in the bookshop and will probably never go back there in her whole entire life. I decide to leave the terminal. It is the only way to find Ma, but then the McFaddens show up and I can't go anywhere.

"Michael, what in the name of God are you doing here?" says Miss Connor, except she isn't Miss Connor anymore. She's Mrs. McFadden.

I remember the lie.

"I was visiting a sick uncle and I ran away to get some sweets when Ma and Da weren't looking and then the train went away without me."

"They didn't wait for you?" says Luke with a frown on his face.

"We were on the train. I jumped off," I say, which is partly true but only a little bit.

"Oh, they must be worried sick," says Mrs. McFadden, who's still Miss Connor in my head.

"They'll be worried all right," says Mr. McFadden, rolling up a cigarette.

"Why are you here?" I ask. "Aren't you supposed to be at your wedding reception?"

"We left early to catch our plane to Greece," smiles Alice.

"It's what honeymooners do," says Luke and in a way that makes me really hate him because Miss Connor gives him a pat on the head for it.

"We're going on a bus," says Alice. "And then we're going on a plane."

"That's great, Alice," I say. She gives me a wide smile. I like her smile.

"What are we going to do with you now?" says Mrs. Mc-Fadden.

"Next train is in twenty minutes, we'll put him on that one. Look at the trouble you've caused now," says Luke, as if he's forty-five years old or something like that.

"What about Ma?" I say without thinking.

"What about her?" says Luke.

"Nothing," I say.

Luke has a funny look on his face. He doesn't believe anything I am saying or he's not sure about what I am saying; neither am I. Suddenly I'm worried Ma will show up and see the new Mrs. McFadden and get all excited and upset, but she doesn't. It is Da and Granny who show up and I am in all kinds of trouble now.

"Michael!" Da yells and I know it's a bad-boy yell and I might not live to be the best soccer player Scotland has ever seen.

Granny has a worried face on her. She's not sure if I will grow up to be the best soccer player Scotland has ever seen either.

"What the hell were you playing at? We had to get off at Cardonald and come all the way back. What's wrong with you, Michael? Stupid boy!" Da smacks the back of my head.

"I wanted some sweets," I say.

Granny and Da look blank.

"Sweets, your arse, you were off to find your ma," snaps Da.

"And why would he be doing that?" says Detective Luke. "Isn't she with you?"

"No, she isn't. She missed the train," says Da.

Da is obviously not prepared for the lie I have told.

"When I said I ran from Ma and Da to get the sweets, I meant my granny and da. Ma missed the train. Isn't that funny?!" I say.

"Hilarious. So where is she?" says Luke.

"How was the wedding, Louisa?" says Granny. "Or should I say Mrs. McFadden? I'll bet it was beautiful."

Granny is changing the subject because that's what people do when other people are in trouble with words and lies and paraphernalia in general.

"Oh, it was the best day of my life, Shirley. I wish you could have been there," says the new Mrs. McFadden.

"How is your brother?" says Mr. McFadden.

"Better," says Granny, whose brother really lives in Canada and never writes or calls on the telephone.

169

"We have to be going now," says Luke, who has luckily become bored of the mysterious train-hopping and my missing ma.

The McFaddens go away and there's a lot of fussing about having a great time and photographs being taken but I can see nothing but rage in Da's face. I'm in for it now, I think.

"Next train is in ten minutes. Let's go," nips Da.

Da walks in front and Granny and I follow him.

When we get on the train no one says one word, but Granny is holding my hand again. She probably feels sorry for me and the hiding I'll get as soon as we get home. I hope the train never moves but as the doors slide closed Ma shows up and through a gap in the door she pushes herself on board.

Everyone is mad at her and no one says hello or even asks where she's been. I wonder if she'll sit next to us at all. She does and right opposite Da.

"I'm sorry, Brian," she says.

Da turns away from Ma to the window. Da is angry and doesn't care one bit how sorry Ma is. He feels he's tried hard with her, as if she's had enough time to be sad and strange, but that feels wrong to me and when she gives me a smile I can see Ma is very tired because of all the trying Da's been doing and maybe if he stopped trying, maybe if we all stopped, then everyone would be happier, especially Ma.

thirty-four

Da was mad when we got home and forgot all about smacking my behind, but I was still sent to bed early. Granny came up to my room with a sandwich but she really wanted to hear the argument Ma and Da were having in their room.

It was wild. There were howls and screams and blaming and tears. Granny says this is how it is when grown-ups want to fix things. Frankie came in my room for a pet. Truth is, he was scared to death. He also needed to pee.

Ma told Da to give her space and stop following her around. Da told Ma to open up. Ma told Da she can't share everything with him and him alone. Da went on about Professor Friendly. Ma threw something. It hit the wall. Da told her to stop chucking things. Then Da said he understood Professor Friendly was just friendly, but he was hurt he wasn't sixty-nine. Granny doesn't know how old Professor Friendly is and neither does Ma. I don't know why it matters at all, but it did matter and Ma told Da he had to have faith in her. She told him Professor Friendly was a great support to her and that made Da upset because he wants to be a support to her; this made Ma tell Da he was a support to her but she needed more support and this made Granny cry because Granny also tries to be a support to her, although Granny couldn't say that because she wasn't even supposed to be listening to who is a support to who. I gave Granny a wee pat on the back and told her she was a great support to us all. This made her happy, but then I am wondering if I am a support to Ma. I think I must be too young to be a support to anyone, but I don't care. I don't want to be a support. I want to play soccer.

Ma asked for time. She asked for space. Da asked, "How much?" Ma didn't say anything or maybe she did and was speaking low. Granny and I couldn't hear her anyway, but then Ma told Da about trust and then Da told Ma about love. It caused a great silence in the end but eventually I was able to get to sleep.

The next day everyone was happy and Da had completely forgotten about meeting the McFaddens and about giving me a tanning. It was brilliant for me until Granny gave me a bowl of porridge and a Valentine's card.

"Must have been slipped through the door after we left for Glasgow," says Granny.

"Michael has a bird," says Da and laughs really hard until Ma reminds him he hasn't gotten her a Valentine's card. It is a close one for Da but then he reminds Ma that it isn't actually Valentine's Day until tomorrow and then he asks her out and in a really cheesy way. He gets down on one knee, takes her hand, and says, "Rosemary Murray, will you have dinner with me?"

The next day Ma and Da decide to have their Valentine's dinner at the Inn, where they always have dinner. Da will have steak with mushrooms because that is what Da likes the best and Ma will have fish. She's mad for fish.

It is a big thing for Ma to go to the Inn because she hasn't been back to the pub since Tricia Law dragged her there last year and made Ma so crazy Kenny's da had to take her to the hospital.

"Get your frock on, girl. It'll be a big night tonight," laughs Granny. "I have a few upstairs from my slimmer days if you want to borrow anything."

"I'll have a look later," says Ma and turns to Da with a wink. Granny's "frocks" will be the last thing Ma will wear stepping out with Da. Poor Granny.

I look at my Valentine's card and someone is not shy and has used their own handwriting. I just need to discover who it belongs to. It's not difficult. I have a look at Alice's poster from the talent show that I kept in my drawer and the writing is exactly the same. This means Alice likes me too, but we are to be quiet on the matter because our families would have a fit if they thought me and Alice were sneaking about together in the bushes, which is what we'll probably do when she comes back from Greece.

I decide I need some chewing gum to prepare my breath for when Alice gets back, and even though I knock, I walk into Ma and Da's room and find Ma taking the pills that make her feel better.

"And what can I do for you tonight, Michael?" she asks.

Ma looks beautiful and I am very proud she is my ma. She is the best-looking of all the mas in town. Her hair has grown longer and she is giving it a little curl with the hot tongs.

"Michael?" she says again.

"I just want some chewing gum," I say.

"You're always in here looking for chewing gum. You need to use some of your pocket money and buy your own."

I want to ask about the pills and that's exactly what I do.

"Will you always take pills, Ma?" I ask.

She stops curling her hair. She thinks of telling me where to get off or maybe to mind my own business, but then she changes her mind and sighs instead.

"I am suffering from anxiety, Michael."

"What's anxiety?" I ask.

"It means I panic at times and for no reason. Like when you're in the Woody alone and someone jumps out of the grass and screams 'Boo' and scares the life out of you."

I nod. "You get a scared feeling like you could be sick."

"That's right, Michael. That feeling you get is called anxiety," says Ma.

"I thought that was fear, Ma."

"It's the same thing, Michael, and these pills, well, they make me less anxious, less fearful."

"Will you always need to take them, Ma? Can you make yourself feel less fearful without them?" I ask.

"I don't know," she says.

"Are you scared of me, Ma?"

She kisses the top of my head.

"What a question," she says. "You're my angel baby and always will be. Why would I be scared of you?"

She is calling me angel baby again and no one except Da and Granny knows she calls me it. It means everything is good again with us and it means Ma is getting a bit more like Ma, but for how long? I wonder. She is so changeable. Granny says we have to take one day at a time.

"Away you go so I can get ready for your da," she says, "and knock before you come in next time," she says.

"I did knock," I say.

"Then knock louder," she says.

When I go downstairs Da is giving his shoes a polish and has slicked his hair back with some kind of wax. He smells of Old Spice because all the ladies love it.

Granny is in a good old mood and has her knitting out. She has given me ten pence for the ice cream van when it comes and we are to have lemonade and maybe some of her fairy cakes with the frosting. I will lick the frosting but shove the cake under the chair. It's going to be a great time. I'll watch TV all night because Granny always falls asleep before she tells me to go to bed and then I'll sneak to bed when I hear Ma and Da come up the stairs.

As things turn out it is me who falls asleep and I am awakened by Da and Ma coming up the stairs outside arguing.

"You didn't need to throw a drink at her is all I'm saying," says Da.

"She was having a go. About you," says Ma. "I wasn't having it."

Granny wakes up. "What's the matter now?"

"Tricia had a go at Brian about being a wife-beater or some damn thing like it and so I threw a gin and tonic at her," says Ma.

I am glad. This means Ma and Tricia Law are not best friends anymore and she won't come here with her fags and her sarcastic remarks at my da.

"Waste of a gin and tonic, as far as I am concerned," says Granny.

"Oh, the lip on that one," says Ma.

Da goes quiet. He's thinking of the truth again and if everyone knew they wouldn't call him a wife-beater at all and there would be no flying drinks, but not wanting to rock the boat he just takes his shoes off and the room smells of beer and feet.

"Any gossip?" says Granny, lighting a cigarette.

"Linda and Kip are going together now," says Ma.

Da tells me to go to bed while Ma and Granny drone about that person and this person and who's doing what to who and all kinds of boring things women talk about. Da falls back in his chair not caring. He falls asleep. I am feeling tired and ready for my bed. I go upstairs without being asked again.

When I go to my room I look out of my window and see Alice's house all dark and empty. I wonder what she's doing in Greece. She's probably found a friend and is playing on a beach somewhere. She's probably all red from the sun, eating expensive chewing gum, and all dirty because she can't help it. They'll be eating all kinds of strange foods in Greece and Luke will be ordering the strangest because he's Luke. Mr. McFadden will order bacon and eggs and maybe the new Mrs. McFadden will order nothing because everything makes her sick these days because of the baby in her belly. I've seen her do it. In the garden once. She almost fainted, but Mr. McFadden caught her and kissed her and took her inside. He's a hero to her. I bet her own wedding cake made her sick.

They will be gone a whole fortnight now and when they get back they will send off their Kodaks for development and weeks later the neighbors will crowd round to see the sun and sand and the red faces they got in Greece. Then the wedding pictures will arrive and there will be more crowding round, people will recognize themselves and compliments will be passed around for lovely shoes and beautiful bags and brilliant dresses. Men won't care and probably won't even look. These are good days for the McFaddens because everyone loves them for being strong and getting on with life, for having parties and weddings. I wonder why it has taken Ma almost a year to get over what has happened to her and why the new Mrs. McFadden took only a few weeks and had a wedding and is about to have a baby and smiles and waves at everyone who walks past her garden. She is always gardening. She and Mr. McFadden are always digging at weeds and clipping at roses. I saw him cut one for her once. He cut it and he handed it to her and she cried and they hugged. I haven't seen the new Mrs. McFadden cry since Woolworths when she found out from Da Patrick Thompson wasn't the man that hurt her in the Woody and that he had been released from prison. The new Mrs. McFadden looks forward to everything and I wonder why Ma can't, but Granny says I am very wrong about that and Ma is dealing with her pain head on. Granny suspects the new Mrs. McFadden is avoiding hers with weddings and gardens, honeymoons and babies.

"She'll come down with a thud eventually and I hope all the love I've seen in that house can save her from it."

I hope Granny is wrong about the "thud" because this "thud" she talks of could be a falling tree and I hope Alice never knows the "thud." I hope she never knows the tears of her da and her new ma. I hope she never knows the fighting and the fear and the sorry words I have heard. I hope the new Mrs. McFadden stays safe and strong for her little baby, but mostly I hope Mr. McFadden will keep the curtains open and not close them like he did last time when he was sad, when Luke had to do the shopping and poor Alice got all dirty with stringy hair. I don't want that for any of them, even Luke, who gets on my nerves for being a lamb and all kinds of gentle creatures.

My granny thinks there is a storm coming for the McFaddens and I don't like my granny for saying it because my ma will have caused that storm and won't know how to calm the waters.

thirty-five

The McFaddens are back. Alice is beautiful and I can't wait to sneak about with her, but her smile is smaller than it was before she left and she looks a little sad to be home. It is raining and so I don't blame her at all. The new Mrs. McFadden is "radiant" according to Granny, and Da can't help notice the "belly on her." Mr. McFadden is rolling his cigarettes and complaining about the food.

"The baby didn't like it either." The new Mrs. McFadden smiles and pats her stomach. "Wherever is your Rosemary?" she says.

"Taking the dog for a walk," I say, which is a good lie until Frankie starts whipping about our legs, showing us all up.

"She must be back," says Da.

"You all look really well. What a beautiful glow you have on you," says Granny.

"Thank you," says the new Mrs. McFadden. "I have a small gift for you all. I'll bring it down later," she says.

"Why don't I pop round to your place?" Granny says, trying to save the day.

Ma cannot see Mrs. McFadden or she'll die of guilt.

"I'll bring a nice cake and we can have a chin-wag."

"Whatever you like," says the new Mrs. McFadden but not

without disappointment. She must notice Ma is never around when she is.

When the rain stops Alice comes out to hang around the Woody with her wellies on.

"Hello," I say.

"Oh hiya," she goes.

She has a stick and she's running it across the grass.

"Did you have a nice holiday?" I ask.

"Obviously," says Alice. She sounds like the old Alice, Dirty Alice, the girl who hates me and not the girl who rolled in the snow with me.

"Make any friends?" I ask.

"Yes," she says.

"That's great," I say.

"A boy. Christos."

"Christos. Sounds like a girl's name."

"Well, it's not," she snaps.

"So what did you do with Christos?" I ask, even though I know what she's going to say. My stomach feels sick with anxiety like Ma's.

"We're friends and we're going to write to each other, like pen pals. We had a good time."

"Is he your boyfriend?"

She doesn't say anything for a minute and then she nods.

"I like you too, Michael, but not like Christos. He's more of a friend. You used to call me Dirty Alice and Christos doesn't even know who Dirty Alice is."

"You're Dirty Alice to me and always will be. So you can fuck off, Dirty Alice. Forever and ever. I'll never say hello to you again and I'll never look at you and I hate you more than anything in the whole world."

Katie Calderwood shows up again. She is dumping a TV and all kinds of stuff. She hears me say "fuck" again.

"Is that you, Michael Murray, saying 'fuck' again and in broad daylight? That's it. I'm going to see your ma."

And off she stomps. Now I know I'm in for it. I walk home feeling sad and angry and fearful like Ma does.

Da answers the door and nods a lot at Katie. They both give me the dirtiest of looks. Katie walks away, shaking her head in disgust. Da drags me indoors. He clips me about the ear. "Don't be saying 'fuck,' you hear me?" I nod.

"Can I go upstairs now?" I say.

"What do you want to go upstairs for?"

"To play or something?"

"Away you go but don't be making any noise and enough with the bad words, OK?" says Da.

"OK," I say.

He goes to the kitchen and I hear him tell Ma and Granny I said "fuck" to Alice. I hear Ma tell Da it's his fault for having a mouth like a sewer. A little fight breaks out about who curses the most. No one wins, although Granny wins a little bit because she goes to church and gets forgiven every Sunday for saying "fuck" and "bastard" and "shithead." Da is forgiven because he sometimes goes to church, but Ma doesn't go to church at all and is chosen as the worst swearer in the house with no one to forgive her.

I go to my room and feel so sad I could cry, but I don't because that would make Dirty Alice the winner of love. I grab a pillow and shove my face into it so no one can hear me and yell, "Fuck! Fuck! Fuck!" I also punch the pillow as if it is her stupid Christos, who stole Dirty Alice from me. Then I see her Valentine's card and her stupid talent show poster sitting side by side and I rip them up into a thousand pieces. I hate her card and I hate her poster. I hate Dirty Alice McFadden and hope she dies.

I am dizzy with all the punching and swearing and thinking of dying and I feel bad I hoped she would die. I don't want Dirty Alice to die but I do want her to fall down or something and break a leg or hurt herself really bad and then she would need help with walking around and I wouldn't help her. I would let her fall.

I feel horrible about Dirty Alice and I don't know what to do and so I go to my ma's room and think I will take one of her pills to make me less anxious and scared and fearful like she does and all the other things that go away when you take one. I sneak into their bedroom.

The pills are in an orange bottle and Ma has left the lid off. They have her name on them. Rosemary Murray. The bottle says "*2 times a day or as needed.*" I think I need a lot and so I pour maybe four into my hand but then I think I see Ma only take one and so I take one for my first try and then another and then another and then another. I put the rest back, that's when Ma shows up and sees me holding her bottle with the lid off. She starts to scream for Da.

"Brian!"

Da knows the scream well and is pounding up the stairs followed by Frankie, who gets kicked out of the way. I hear him yelp.

"What's going on?" yells Granny.

"He's taken the pills. Oh dear God," says Ma.

"How many did you take?" growls Da. He grabs at the bottle. He checks the contents. "Michael, for the love of Jesus, how many did you take?" He grabs my mouth, opens it, and can see I've already swallowed whatever I've taken.

"Two. Three," I cry. "I don't know."

"We have to get him to the hospital," says Ma.

"Call Kenny's da," says Granny.

Ma runs down the stairs followed by Frankie. She almost trips on him. "Would someone throw that fucking dog outside?!" yells Ma.

Granny runs down and throws Frankie out the back, saving him from careless feet and boots up the arse.

I start to feel sleepy and my mouth feels dry. My legs go wobbly. I have to sit on the ground.

"Get up, Michael. Get up!" yells Da.

Da lifts me into his arms. "Stay awake, son," but I can't.

The next thing I remember is throwing up into a bucket and I have a tube in my nose. It feels horrible and it hurts. I hear Ma crying like a baby and when I look up I see Da and Granny looking worried and a doctor looking angry. He is the new doctor. We call him Dr. Mainland because he's from the mainland and everyone hates him. Everyone preferred Dr. Robertson, but he retired last year and is now living with his sister in Glasgow. He had been our family doctor for my whole life and gave us all lollipops whenever we want to see him.

"You can't leave those things lying around. That's what medicine cabinets are for," growls Dr. Mainland.

Paula Leighton, who Ma went to school with, is the nurse

helping with the tube removal and silver buckets of vomit. She smiles awkwardly at Ma.

"Will he be OK?" Ma asks Paula.

"He will," whispers Paula.

"It's fortunate for us all he didn't take the whole bottle. I am referring this case to the social services. There's something very wrong here. I've seen this boy twice in the past year and I am concerned for his welfare."

Dr. Mainland scribbles something on his clipboard.

"He took a few pills by mistake," says Da. "What's the big deal?"

"And what I want to know is why? He's twelve years old. He can read. He must have known what was in the bottle was forbidden. I'm sure you told him at some stage during usage."

"I was suffering from anxiety," I croak.

"Anxiety? You see, this is what I'm talking about. What does a twelve-year-old have to be anxious about and what does he know about the word anyway? It's not right. These pills are your responsibility and they're certainly not something I'd prescribe."

"I get them from Greenock," says Ma.

"Greenock?"

"My doctor is in Greenock," says Ma.

Dr. Mainland is suspicious. "It's a very strong drug and the dosage is high. May I ask why?"

Dr. Mainland pauses at Ma's red face.

Ma looks to Da, to Granny, to the doctor, and finally to Paula Leighton. She sighs.

"I was raped."

Dr. Mainland's face changes color and I'm glad.

"Would you like Nurse Leighton to take your son into another room, Mrs. Murray?" he asks and in a voice very different from the one he had been using on us before.

"Michael knows everything. He shouldn't know but he does. He can stay." Ma gives me a gentle look as if she's sorry for everything in the whole wide world. I want to tell her it's OK. Telling is for the best. Dr. Mainland looks uncomfortable. I want to snigger at him for trying to send me away like I'm some big baby when I know it all.

"I was coming home from work. I took a shortcut through the park and that's where he attacked me. I was in the hospital here. I was badly beaten. There are pictures in my medical file. I made everyone think my husband did it, but he didn't. It was a dirty bastard crawling through the park looking for stupid women like me taking shortcuts in the dark. I got the pills from a doctor in Greenock. They help me sleep."

Da sits on a nearby chair as if he might faint or something. I am stuck on a gurney with Granny holding my hand.

The promise has been broken, but Ma is the one who broke it. The secret is out.

"Does anyone else know?" asks Dr. Mainland and with a true gentleness in his voice.

Ma shakes her head.

"Did this rape happen before or after Louisa McFadden's attack?" asks Paula.

"Before, a long time before," says Ma.

"Then why didn't you come forward?" snips Paula. She's all frost now.

"I was afraid," hushes Ma.

"Afraid?" says Paula. "We've all been afraid. Every woman on this island has been terrified to death."

"That will be enough, Nurse Leighton, you can leave now," says Dr. Mainland.

Nurse Paula leaves and with a bit of drama on her heels. Da holds Ma's hand.

Dr. Mainland taps his pen on the clipboard. "You know you have to tell the police, Mrs. Murray."

Ma nods and for the first time since the attack she does not cry when talking about it. Her heart is strong. Her mind is able. She is ready to tell. It's over, I think. My ma has told the truth and everyone will know my da is not a wife-beater and what happened to Mrs. McFadden also happened to my ma, but I am also afraid because Ma should have told sooner than this. She should have warned people and she didn't; now I don't know what will happen.

thirty-six

Ma and Da come home late from the police station and miss their dinner. I am with Granny drinking hot chocolate in the kitchen because I have been in the hospital and can do what I like.

Granny makes them something to eat straightaway. Ma and Da tell her a special policeman from the mainland came over to talk to them. I can tell Ma and Da are very tired. No one even minds I am there and I am very quiet because I don't want to remind them. It is a sad story they tell and I don't know who to feel bad for the most because when Ma left the police station Mrs. McFadden was waiting with Mr. McFadden. They were being interviewed too about the rapist, but when Mrs. McFadden sees my ma she walks right over to her and slaps her hard in the face.

"She did not," screams Granny.

" 'We've all suffered here,' I told her," says Da. " 'Fuck you, Brian,' McFadden says to me. 'No one else would have suffered at all if your Rosemary had just told the truth. Women on this island would have known to keep themselves safe and my Louisa would never have been attacked. Shame on you, Rosemary Murray. Shame.' "

"And who is he to talk of shame when he was living in sin with a pregnant woman?" yells Granny.

"Don't, Shirley. It's not the same," says Ma.

Ma sits down and reaches for the teapot. She pours Da a cup and then herself. Her hands are shaking. She offers the pot to Granny but Granny has had enough tea while she was waiting for them to come home and tell us the news. She pees a lot. Ma and Da both look like they have something to say but it's Ma who says it.

"They have him," says Ma.

"Have who?" says Granny.

"The rapist. Who do you think?" nips Da.

I am shocked to death.

"Up in Glasgow. He's killed two prostitutes already and left one barely alive. I've to go to Glasgow and identify him."

"And did the police tell anyone about the prostitutes? No, they fucking didn't!" screams Granny.

"It was in Glasgow, Shirley. No one knew he'd come here."

Da rubs his face with his hands.

"It's the gold bracelet, you know. They kept going on about it. The weight of it. The feel of it. Then they brought out lots of other bracelets for me to look at."

"Did you see it, Rosemary?" says Granny.

Ma nods her head. "I did. It had charms on it."

The doorbell rings. It is Tricia Law on the doorstep. She knows everything on account of Nurse Paula Leighton being her first cousin and unable to keep her trap shut. Tricia grabs at Ma and hugs her like mad.

"You should have told me," cries Tricia.

"I couldn't tell anyone," cries Ma.

Tricia stops hugging Ma and turns her attentions to Da.

"Why didn't you say something?" nips Tricia. "I could have helped her."

"How?" yells Da. He turns from Tricia and heads to the living room. He has no time for Tricia Law anymore. I don't blame him. Tricia breaks up families and fights with short skirts and black knickers at parties. Worse than that, she comes to your house and almost spits in your da's eye.

"I brought you some Juicy Fruit, Michael," says Tricia. I take the chewing gum but I don't say thank you or give her a big smile like I used to. I follow my da and close the door behind me.

Granny makes her excuses and takes Frankie for a walk, which is a huge excuse for Granny because she never takes Frankie anywhere. I don't even think she knows how, but Frankie won't care. He'll hurl himself in front of her and with her little legs Granny will have to catch up to him. I wish I was going just to watch but I'd rather sit with Da and chew my gum.

Tricia stays for a long time with Ma. She is probably another support to Ma and Ma needs a lot of support right now, even if it is from Tricia Law who Ma threw gin at the week before. Tricia and Ma are best friends whether we like it or not and so we say nothing and hide from their friendship. Da says women are funny when it comes to being friends.

"They can fight and love and all in the same breath," says Da. "Always stay clear of women having a go at each other and NEVER get involved."

Da says Ma might have to go to Glasgow High Court and give evidence and face the dirty rapist again. She will need her family and her friends around her, maybe Professor Friendly will come. Tricia will definitely come, but not me. I'll be left in Rothesay with Granny. Tricia will go to the High Court and not care about Da or Granny not liking her.

"She has a thick skin, that one," says Granny.

When Tricia leaves the house she sticks her head around the living room door and says good-bye to Da, who hates the bones of her, but Tricia will keep saying good-bye to Da until she dies because that is how Tricia is.

"See you around, Michael," she says and gives me a wink, which means she will always have Juicy Fruit for me. I wink back because I want the Juicy Fruit.

"It's going to be tough, Michael, you know that, don't you?" says Da.

I nod.

"People will say things about your ma and you have to turn the other cheek, you understand?"

"I will, Da."

"You just ignore them, son," says Granny.

"What about you, Ma?" I ask.

"I won't mind them. None of us will."

But that's not what happened.

thirty-seven

Everyone on the bus was noisy but then I got on and the place got quiet. I notice the driver snatch a look at me through the rear-view mirror.

"Sit on your arse, boy," he says.

I realize then the driver is Suzanne Miller's father and he looks ready to burst open at the sight of me.

It wasn't me, I want to say to him. It wasn't me who lied and kept secrets. It was my ma.

Walking up the aisle, I see Paul on one side of the bus and he's sitting next to Fat Ralph.

"All right, Michael?" says Fat Ralph.

"Fine," I say to Fat Ralph.

Paul just nods at me and then looks through the window. I should bash his brains in for that, but he has lots of power today. Everyone on the bus has. They are all together and I am on my own. They have been told by their parents to stay away from the Murrays. We've done a terrible thing and everything about us is wrong. My ma kept a secret that got Mrs. McFadden hurt and ruined. It is lucky Mrs. McFadden is alive today, they say. No one cares the same is true of my ma, that she could also have been killed.

Nothing much is being said to me because I am still the toughest lad in the housing estate and it seems to keep the bus silent.

Dirty Alice is at the back of the bus with Marianne, Tracey, and Fiona. She looks at me like she could kill me, but there is another look in her face and it means something else.

I sit down and hope the bus stays quiet but I know someone is going to say something.

Da says every house in the estate has been jabbering about my ma and there's no point guessing or worrying about it. "It's done," he says.

Maybe some people will feel bad for her, I think. Maybe some people will blame her. Maybe some people won't care about it at all and won't want to be involved, but on an island like this someone will be thinking something and when people are thinking they are also looking and it's the looking that scares Ma the most. She says it speaks the loudest.

"Your ma is a stupid bitch," says Dirty Alice.

Everyone looks up. A fight, they think, a grand old fight, but I will never fight Dirty Alice.

"Shut your mouth, you filthy cow," I say.

"I will not. Your ma didn't tell the police what happened to her. If your ma had told them, what happened to my ma wouldn't have happened at all."

"Your ma?" I laugh, but I don't mean to. I'm just trying to show how strong I am and that Dirty Alice is just stupid.

"Leave it alone, Alice," says Luke, who is reading a book two seats up. I didn't even see him at first, but when he sees me, he looks away like Paul did and stares out of the window as if I don't exist.

"That's right, my ma," says Dirty Alice and she's daring me to say otherwise but I don't. I just want to sit back down again and look out of the window like Luke and Paul. I want to forget this whole thing.

"Why don't you just shut up? You don't know anything about anything," I say, and I turn my back to her and sit on my seat.

"Make me," she says.

I can't believe it; Dirty Alice wants to fight me now and on a bus driven by Suzanne Miller's da who hates me too.

Suzanne Miller's da should stop the bus. It's not like he didn't hear a girl wants to fight the toughest boy in the estate, but he doesn't care because maybe he wants a fight and hopes the whole bus will jump on top of me. I worry they might.

Dirty Alice sits behind me then. She smells of Bazooka Joe bubblegum. I turn to her with a face on me. I need to pretend I hate her and don't want her anywhere near me. Her skin is still brown from her holiday. Her hair is shiny and her skin looks soft. I hope she will change her mind about being nasty to me and be nice like she was before. I hope she remembers the Valentine's card she sent, but she doesn't. She grabs at my hair and slaps me across the face like Mrs. McFadden slapped my ma. I don't hit her back because she is a girl and because she is Dirty Alice. She jumps on top of me then and punches me until my nose bleeds. The blood makes me afraid and angry. I want to reach for her long hair and pound her head off my fist. I want to pull her from the seat and kick her up and down the aisle, but I don't. I let the blood melt. I let the tears boil and fall down my face. I look straight into her eyes, my face red and bruised. I see the hurt in her then, I see the Valentine's card, but she won't cry, not Dirty Alice. She doesn't like me anymore and we are back to how it was before. Hate.

"Fucking pussy," she says loudly and returns to the back of the bus with a victorious smile on her face. The girls yell, "Championnnn, championnnn!"

I cry then. I cry for the blood. I cry because I am alone. I cry because I am no longer the toughest lad in the estate and because a girl called Alice McFadden kicked the arse out of me. I will never be tough again.

thirty-eight

M a goes to Glasgow to identify the rapist with Da. Tricia
Law also comes and drives Da mad with her gabbing.
Mrs. McFadden won't go. She is afraid to admit she made a
mistake about Patrick Thompson, who has left the island and
can't come back anymore.

Da tells Granny in the kitchen Ma was brave and faced
the pervert head on and not behind a sheet of glass, but Ma
couldn't make her mind up between two men, both of them
with red hair. She chose the one who smelled of smoke. It was
the right choice and the same one Suzanne Miller made, although they don't exactly hug about it on the boat home. Da
tells us everything while Ma stirs her tea and hardly says a
thing. It was a big day for her but Suzanne Miller was mad at
her and told her so in front of the whole ferry.

" 'He could have raped me,' she said, and with everyone
watching us, Ma," says Da. "But then Tricia reminds the stupid girl that he didn't rape her."

"No, he didn't," says Granny. "And she should count her
lucky stars, little bitch."

"Don't, Shirley," says Ma.

" 'But he terrified the life out of me,' she says. 'I still can't go out on my own,' she tells us, and I swear, Ma, the dirty looks they were giving us on that boat."

"Can you blame them?" says Ma.

"And how do they think it was for you, Rosemary?" says Da, who is getting very worked up about it all.

"And what about the prostitute?" asks Granny. "What's she saying?"

"We don't know," says Ma.

"It won't matter anyway," says Granny.

"Why not, Granny?" I ask.

"She's a lady of the night. The bad sort," says Granny.

"A prostitute?" I ask.

Granny nods.

"What's a prostitute?" I ask.

"Never you mind," Granny says.

"But you're always talking about them," I say.

"I am not," says Granny.

"You say it about everyone." And she does. If a woman has a short skirt on her. If a woman wears tight trousers. If a woman has bleached hair. If a woman wears too much makeup and if she sees a woman talking to a man she isn't married to, Granny goes mad about it and calls her a prostitute. Granny even called Mrs. McFadden a prostitute when she was Miss Connor and going to the pub with Mr. McFadden.

Da laughs his head off. "Boy's right," he says.

Granny is annoyed. "You shut up," she says to Da.

"No, you shut up," says Da to Granny.

"Both of you shut up," says Ma and then tells me what a prostitute is. I am shocked to death that Granny would call anyone we know a prostitute, especially Mrs. McFadden.

"I still don't understand why it will be hard to get the man who hurt you in jail, Ma, because one of the other women is a prostitute. She saw him just like you did."

"I don't know either," says Ma.

"The truth is, Michael, it's going to be hard convincing a jury that a man raped any woman," says Da.

"But why?" I ask.

"Because that's how it is in the world," whispers Ma. "And it might never change."

"You're wrong, Ma. The judge will see how horrible he is and he'll put him away forever and ever."

Da puts his hand on Ma's back then. She's drinking tea and looking sad, but no tears come. Ma isn't crying too much these days, or maybe she is, I just never see her.

thirty-nine

Ma and Da go everywhere together. He couldn't save her from the rapist but he can save her from wagging tongues and dirty looks. Of course not everyone gives her dirty looks, some people are very nice and hug her in the street. They ask if there is anything they can do but it is way too late for that now. Other people just smile at her because they have their own business to be getting on with.

Da says the only way forward is to get out there and confront the demon that is gossip and not to hide like a criminal but to face the angry people head on.

"We won't run away from this, Rosemary. What's done is done!"

Ma nods and listens to Da for the first time in ages. They take Frankie on long walks to the loch or on the shore road and I go along too, but sometimes I don't. People stare and it puts me off enjoying my ma and da's company. Anyway, I have my keepy-uppies to practice.

Granny is quiet about it all and goes to chapel all the time, cleaning the pews and arranging the flowers. She even knitted the priest a cardigan. It made Mrs. Maitland mad with jealousy because she wants to clean the pews and arrange the flowers too and so the priest says they must share the duties of God, who likes really shiny chairs and beautiful carnations.

"The priest is a great counselor of sin," says Granny, who feels very badly for the secret we have kept. We all do, but like Da says, there is nothing to be done about it now, not even if you're being beaten on a bus driven by Suzanne Miller's da.

"Everyone has a fucking opinion. Today it's this. Tomorrow it will be something else. We have the bastard is the main thing," yells Da, who has started to yell about everything to do with the pervert who hurt Ma, so does Tricia Law. It's the one thing they have in common and together they yell their heads off about judges and juries and ignorance.

"Tricia is a lion," says Granny, who likes her much more now she's gobbing off at Ma's workmates for saying Ma did wrong not telling anyone what happened to her in the park, but Ma doesn't care about them. Ma only cares about Louisa McFadden. Ma is desperate to talk to her but Da says it is a bad idea.

"There is nothing to be mended there, Rosemary," he says.

"Brian's right," says Granny. "Leave the woman be."

Sometimes I find Ma peeking through the curtains in her bedroom at Mrs. McFadden sitting in the garden holding on to her big belly.

"Rosemary, get away from that window," says Da, catching her spying on Mrs. McFadden. I'm glad he never caught me when she was Miss Connor.

"But we're in the same boat," says Ma to him.

"Rosemary, that poor woman wouldn't be in our boat at all if we'd all just said something. We did her wrong. She's not going to fall into your arms for that."

Ma nods and cries with the guilt and Da holds her tight.

forty

The rain comes in May. A terrible rain. The kind you can hear on the roof. The kind that hits concrete like a stone. The kind that blinds you and smacks you in the face like it hates you. The kind you get lost in.

Mr. McFadden went off to the mainland in the morning to get a surprise for Mrs. McFadden and the baby. That's what Mrs. Maitland told Granny anyway and Granny was annoyed at her because Mrs. Maitland knows of the situation between the Murray family and the McFaddens, everyone does, and Granny hates to be reminded.

"She was trying to cause some trouble. And in a house of God. Old bitch."

When the electricity goes off because of the storm I get very excited. We always have brilliant food when there is a power cut. Granny brings out pickles, cheese, yogurts, and crackers and jam, anything she doesn't have to cook, which is brilliant. Granny also brings out her scones, even though we'll get indigestion if we eat them, but if we don't we will hurt her feelings and so we spread jam on them and nibble at the edges.

The doorbell rings and it's Dirty Alice with a broken umbrella. We are all very surprised to see her. Her face is red from the rain and she looks very scared. I am glad she is scared and I hope she might cry so I can tell everyone what a whiner she is.

"My ma is having the baby," she yells and everyone is still. Granny doesn't say anything, just grabs for her coat. Everyone knows Granny was a nurse. She was a very famous nurse on the island.

"I've wiped a lot of arses around this town," she says.

Granny doesn't have time for umbrellas or scarves. She only cares for Mrs. McFadden.

"I should come," says Ma, grabbing for her jacket.

"No," says Granny and she's very firm with Ma.

Ma steps away from the coatrack, where all kinds of jackets and hats are hung.

Granny runs out the door to Mrs. McFadden and leaves Ma all worried and wanting to help. Da takes Ma's hands.

"If she needs you she'll call for you," says Da. "Let's go bin the scones before she comes back."

Ma doesn't laugh and neither do I. We feel frightened for Mrs. McFadden and Da's joke is stupid anyway.

A long time passes eating cucumbers and yogurts. Ma stares sadly out the window at the McFadden house. She doesn't even see Dirty Alice running toward us until she's banging like a madwoman on our front door.

"The baby is coming. You have to come help my ma. Shirley says so. My ma's screaming her head off."

I want my ma to say no, but since it's Dirty Alice's ma who is screaming and not Dirty Alice, I'm glad my ma grabs for her coat.

"You stay here, Alice," says Ma.

"I will not," says Dirty Alice.

201

"You can't help anyone at the house," says Ma.

"You can't tell me what to do!" screams Dirty Alice. "My da will go mental if he finds out you've crossed our doorstep."

"Then why are you here?" asks Da angrily.

"Because there's no one else to ask and Michael's granny says so."

"Then do as you're told," screams Ma and then rushes out the door in a great fury.

This scares Dirty Alice and I'm glad. She can't talk to my ma like that. No way!

"Maybe you should go, Da?" I say.

"No, son, best leave the baby stuff to the women," he says.

"But I'm a woman," says Dirty Alice.

"You're a little girl," I say.

"Not too little to kick your head in," she snaps at me.

"That's enough of that, wee miss," says Da. "Go into the bathroom and grab yourself a towel, then come into the living room for a bite to eat."

"I'm not hungry," says Dirty Alice.

"You'll have a little bit of something," says Da.

And she does. She practically eats us out of house and home. She even eats Granny's scones. She must have been starving to death.

The next thing Luke comes rushing to the door and tells Da he has to come. It's a busy night.

"I don't think that's right, Luke," says Da.

"Don't be a baby," says Luke and like a very serious little woman. "It's a desperate situation. She's in agony. I can't be fetching water and keeping her cool at the same time. She's sweating buckets and Rosemary has to sit behind her for support."

"For Jesus' sake," says Da and then goes for his coat, but not as fast as Ma or Granny.

"What about us?" says Dirty Alice.

"Stay here," says Luke.

"I don't want to stay with him," says Dirty Alice.

"I don't want to stay with her," I say.

"Oh, behave yourself, the pair of you," says Luke. "This is important. Your little drama will have to wait."

They run off and leave me with Dirty Alice and Frankie. Frankie is friendly. I am not. I don't say a word. I hate her and suddenly I hate Frankie.

We just sit there until Dirty Alice, *capital D*, says to my amazement, "I am sorry I kicked your head in."

I want to slap her face for that but I say, "You only won because I let you. Boys can't hit girls."

"If they're tough they can," she says.

"Shut up," I say.

"I hate you," she screams. "And I don't want to stay here with you. My ma is having a baby and I want to see what happens," she says.

"Me too," I say and stand up to get my coat.

"You can't come to my house," she says.

"All my family is at your house," I say.

"They shouldn't be there either. My dad will go mad."

"We're helping your fat ma have a baby. He'll have to lump it," I say.

"Fine. Come," she yells. "See if I care. God, you're so immature."

I hate her for saying this word. "Immature." All the girls are saying it right now, like they're big women or something and all the boys are little lads, but I hate it the most because Dirty Alice has said it. I should call her a daft cow but I don't. We have to go see Mrs. McFadden have her baby and that is more important. I wonder if stupid Christo's still her boyfriend.

When we get to Dirty Alice's door we are red in the face and soaked right through. It's crazy weather. The whole housing estate is pitch black, all the lights are off, all the telephone lines are down, and everyone is huddling in the dark in their houses hoping the lights will come back on, especially the McFaddens.

Luke opens the door and all we can hear is poor Mrs. McFadden screaming like a madwoman.

"What are you both doing here?"

"It's my house too," says Dirty Alice and pushes through Luke like he's a breeze. I wait first. I don't like the idea of barging about the place like Dirty Alice does and the screaming is scaring me.

"I suppose you'd better come in," says Luke. "Go into the living room and wait there. Do not come upstairs or I'll go mental."

I wonder what that might look like but I do as I am told.

I have never been in Dirty Alice's house and it is very clean. She even has brown-and-orange wallpaper and it feels like felt.

"Don't touch my walls," nips Dirty Alice. "Don't know where your hands have been."

"I let you eat our food," I say.

"I don't care, stop touching things," she says.

I put my hands in my pockets while Mrs. McFadden screams all kinds of things. I hear Granny telling her to let it all out. I hear doors opening and closing. I hear footsteps walking across the landing and thumping down the stairs, but no one comes into the room. I am trapped in it with Dirty Alice.

Their living room is very nice, I think to myself. Mrs. McFadden has made it all lovely because she is lovely. It has more furniture than her last house and she has plenty of ornaments. She likes people in old-fashioned clothes and angels. She also has china dogs. I like the dogs the best because they are very happy and they're chewing on bones and things.

Da comes in and he's sweating and looking very ill.

"What are you both doing here?" he asks.

"Alice made me come," I say.

"And if Alice told you to jump in the Clyde, would you?"

Dirty Alice thinks this is hilarious and it makes me annoyed at Da.

"How is my ma?" says Dirty Alice.

"She's fine. She's fine," says Da, rubbing his neck with a cloth.

The screaming gets louder.

"She doesn't sound fine to me," says Dirty Alice.

"That's what it sounds like when women have their babies. They're very noisy and say all kinds of things, but then the baby comes and they're all back to being nice."

"Why is it taking so long?" says Dirty Alice. "I want to see the baby."

"Baby is taking its time. It has a big head so it's very uncomfortable."

"How big?" I say.

"I don't know, it's what Granny says. She's trying to pull the thing out of her."

"Did you see?" says Dirty Alice.

"Indeed I did not, that's no place for a man to be."

"Then what are you doing up there?" says Dirty Alice.

"I am wiping the sweat from her brow," says Da.

"So what are you doing in here?"

"Toilet break."

"Then you must be lost because this is the living room," says Dirty Alice.

"You're quite the little madam, aren't you, with all these questions, Alice?" says Da and with a curl in his voice.

"What is Luke doing?" I ask.

"He's a good boy, that Luke," says Da.

"But what's he doing?" I say.

"Everything he can," says Da.

Ma yells for Da. He has to go back but you can tell he'd rather stay and touch the wallpaper, maybe admire the happy dogs, and never go upstairs again.

"I have to go now," says Da and before long he is thumping up the stairs to where Mrs. McFadden is having the baby with the big head.

"Let's go look," says Dirty Alice.

"We're not allowed," I say.

"Who cares what they say. Come on."

I don't want to go. I am afraid. I don't want to see a lady have a baby, especially a lady who used to be Miss Connor and danced in her bedroom.

"OK," I say and follow Dirty Alice to the stairs. When we get to the top, the door is wide open. I see Granny kneeling with Luke at her side and yelling, "Louisa, you're doing great, give it plenty," but poor Mrs. McFadden is crying because she can't. Da is wiping her forehead and Ma is sitting behind her and holding her tight. Ma is telling Mrs. McFadden that she can do it, that she can get the baby out of her. There is blood everywhere and Mrs. McFadden's legs are wide open. I feel sick and wish I was blind. I run away, but Dirty Alice stays until Luke pushes her out of the room and shuts the door. Dirty Alice is raging and bangs on the door but nobody cares.

"I hate him. Acts like he knows it all," says Dirty Alice.

I feel ill at what I have seen. I want to go home through the rain and to Frankie and the pickles.

That's when Mr. McFadden walks through the door. He took the emergency boat from Gourock and is back in time to hear Mrs. McFadden screaming like a banshee.

"What the hell is he doing here?" says Mr. McFadden, who is wet to the bone and deaf as a post.

"Ma is having her baby and the stupid Murrays are helping us," says Dirty Alice.

When Da arrives at the top of the stairs Mr. McFadden is not pleased to see him either.

"What the fuck is all this?" Mr. McFadden snarls.

"What do you think it is? Can't you hear, man?"

"Of course I can fucking hear. What are you doing up there?"

"I don't fucking know," says Da.

Mr. McFadden has lots of bags and drops them at the door. He runs up the stairs as quickly as he can and then comes out as fast as he went in.

"Maybe I should wait here," says Mr. McFadden, who is like Da when it comes to the baby with the big head, but then Mrs. McFadden starts screaming for him.

"I'll go home then," says Da and goes downstairs, leaving

Mr. McFadden to hate us on his own, but Da doesn't even get to the bottom of the stairs before the baby is here and starts to cry.

Mr. McFadden goes to Mrs. McFadden and Dirty Alice gallops like a horse to where her new ma and the baby are.

"Let's go, Michael," says Da.

"You don't want to see the baby, Da?" I ask.

"That's enough for me and babies tonight."

As we walk out the door the lights come back on. The power cut is over and it almost hurts your eyes with the brightness of it.

An hour later Ma comes home without Granny, who went to the hospital with the McFaddens.

"Girl or boy?" Da asks Ma.

"Little girl," she says. "They've named her Amanda."

"Was she mad you were there?" asks Da.

"I don't think she noticed," says Ma.

"I'm sure she did," says Da.

"You think she'll give me a medal?"

"You were at hand to help, it counts for something," says Da.

"I hope so," says Ma, but you can tell she's not sure if it should.

forty-one

Mrs. McFadden brings home the baby with the big head. Mr. McFadden is very proud and goes for a spin around the block with the big pram he ordered from the mainland. It's like a car with a huge hood; it has silver handles and big wheels. A whole boy could sit in it.

Mrs. McFadden is in bed. She is having difficulty moving around after the birth of her baby.

"Terrible tears she's had," says Granny.

Granny visits regularly and helps Mrs. McFadden get in and out of baths.

Ma doesn't ask Granny if Mrs. McFadden has mentioned her but you can tell she is dying to. Granny says nothing to Ma about the goings-on in the McFadden house. Dirty Alice goes around the estate telling all kinds of lies though and I hear her.

"I saw it with my own eyes," she told Marianne.

"Did you see the blood? My ma says it is a bloody thing to have a baby."

"Oh, it was everywhere, but I helped my ma as best as I could," says Dirty Alice.

"I think you could be a nurse or something, Alice," beams Marianne.

"I could," says Dirty Alice.

I do my keepy-uppies. I should show her up but then she would tell everyone about how white I went at the sight of her ma's legs spread wide with a baby squeezing out of them. I would hate that.

Tricia Law comes round the corner. Tricia is always around these days and trying her best to keep Ma's mind off all the things she has to think about, like the court case and Mrs. McFadden. Tricia is a good friend and we are secretly happy she is around for Ma's sake.

Professor Friendly also comes and brings good news. Ma has passed her exams. Da is not too pleased to see him but hides it well. He even makes Professor Friendly a cup of tea and Granny tries to make him eat her scones, but he is allergic to flour and doesn't have to eat one bite. Professor Friendly tells Ma she could be a teacher. Granny and Da are very impressed.

"A teacher?" Da says.

"I don't know," says Ma, who doesn't believe she can be anyone except the woman walking alone in the park at night.

"That would be great, Ma. You can be my teacher and never give me homework," I say.

"You'd like that all right," laughs Da.

"It would be a four-year training course, Rosemary, but I know you could do it. What do you think?"

"Can I think on it?" she says to Professor Friendly.

Professor Friendly tells her she has all the time in the world but he also tells her to have faith in herself and her abilities.

"You are a star student," he tells Ma and this makes her happy.

Granny goes off to Mrs. McFadden for a while and when she gets back there is a box of chocolates on the table. It is from Mrs. McFadden. To Ma.

Ma doesn't know what to do with herself. The card says "To Rosemary, thank you" and it bothers Ma. She wants Mrs. McFadden to say something like "Rosemary, come and visit me and we'll forget the whole thing" but that's not what Mrs. McFadden says. She just says "thank you." I don't care about it all. I am too excited for the chocolates, but Ma won't let anyone touch them for a while, it's as if she's been given a china plate instead of a box of Milk Tray. I am annoyed.

"Should I pop by to see the baby?" Ma asks.

Granny shakes her head. "One step at a time," she says.

This makes Ma irritated at Granny, but she doesn't say too much about it and puts on a sulky face instead.

"Where are you going, Shirley?" Ma says to Granny, who has her jacket on and is holding a grocery bag.

"The shops, where do you think? We need bread and milk."

From the window Ma watches Granny go down the hill to the shop and then grabs for her own coat.

"Can I have a chocolate now?" I ask.

"Sure, Michael," she says.

She removes the wrapper and gently lifts the purple lid of the most beautiful box in the whole world. I take a nice toffee chocolate. They're chewy and last longer.

"I'm taking Frankie for a walk," says Ma.

"I'll come," I say.

"No, you're all right, Michael, stay and guard the chocolates." Ma is smiling.

"How many can I have?" I ask.

"Three," says Ma.

"Four," I say.

"All right, four," says Ma and gives me a wink. It's the best day ever. I'm eating my chocolates and having a great old time until Frankie appears at my legs wanting a chocolate too.

I look out the door for Ma and that is when I see her walking toward the McFadden house. Da is sleeping on the sofa and I wonder if I should wake him, but I don't. If Mrs. McFadden doesn't want Ma anywhere near her, then she'll tell Ma straight and yell for her to get away from her front door, but if Mrs. McFadden is OK with it, then Ma can go inside her house and they can talk about the thing they both secretly want to talk about. The man in the park. The man in the Woody.

It is Mr. McFadden who answers the door and he is shocked to death to see Ma. He is frowning and says something I can't hear. Maybe Ma says something else but I don't know because her back is to me. Then Mr. McFadden disappears for a minute, but leaves Ma to linger on the doorstep. It is obvious Mr. McFadden is going to ask Mrs. McFadden if she will talk to the woman who ruined her life, but who also helped deliver baby Amanda. Mr. McFadden comes back and shakes his head at Ma. Then he closes the door on her. Ma walks away, but then the door opens again and it is Mrs. McFadden this time and she is yelling for Ma to come back. Ma rushes back up the hill and walks through the McFadden doorway. I see Dirty Alice at her window and she's looking right at me. She gives me two fingers and then disappears behind the curtain. God, I hate her.

Ma stays at the McFadden house for a long time. I wonder if they have murdered her or something.

Granny comes back from the shops and asks where Ma is. I say nothing and shrug my shoulders. Da wakes up and asks what's for dinner. Granny produces fish and chips. I am thrilled. It has to be the best dinner in the world.

Then Ma comes home. She is bright and cheery. It has been a good visit, I think. She winks at me. I know her secret. It's an OK secret to have though and I'm not too bothered, also I want the rest of the chocolates.

We have our suppers in the paper with a bottle of fizzy juice. Ma eats everything. Granny says something about her appetite coming back. Da looks thrilled.

"I have a surprise," he says.

I hope it's ice cream from the van.

"What is it, Da?"

"I have a job," he says.

Everyone is stunned and we don't believe him for a minute.

"Doing what?" says Granny.

"They're rebuilding the pier," says Da. "Skinny Rab put in a good word for me. You're talking to an employed man now."

Ma gives Da a huge hug and almost knocks Da's chips to the ground.

"Fortune's smiling on us now," says Granny.

"It is, Ma," says Da.

Everyone is happy. Ma is speaking to Mrs. McFadden, Da has a job, and Mrs. Maitland has broken her hip and can't help in the chapel anymore, making Granny the priest's number-one girl. It is a good day for the Murrays.

"What did you say to Mrs. McFadden?" I ask Ma when we are alone.

Ma puts her finger to her lips and says, "Shhhhhhh, Michael! Not a word to anyone."

Ma disappears upstairs to Da and I wonder if Dirty Alice knows. She listens through doors like I do. I'm sure of it.

forty-two

It's been raining hard and for days. When it stops I am dying to get out and play. Dirty Alice is in the Woody and sulking like a madwoman. She is as filthy as ever, her socks wet with mud and rain. She doesn't even have a jacket on and it's freezing out.

"What's the matter with you?" I ask.

"Never you mind, Michael *stupid* Murray." She throws the stick she's holding into the grass.

"You're a right moaner, Alice, you know that?" I say.

She doesn't argue.

Next thing she's crying all over the place. I wish someone else could see her and then we could laugh at her together, but it's only me in the Woody. She doesn't even care I'm standing there and won't stop blubbering. I've heard her cry before but only after a fall or that time I threw a rock at her head. It was tiny, but she bawled like crazy. I think I should walk away and leave her to her tears, but she's choking on them and her face is drenched in snot. I don't even have a hanky. She doesn't care anyway and wipes all the teary goo from her face with her elbow. She's disgusting, that Alice.

"What's wrong with you?" I ask.

"My ma and da only care about baby Amanda."

"Is that all?" I say. "Grow up and don't be so immature."

Immature, I think. It is a good word.

"Luke's the same. It's all Amanda this and Amanda that. I'm not even allowed to hold her in case I drop her."

"Maybe you would. You're always falling about the place," I say.

"I would not," she cries.

I don't know what to say to her now. Maybe she wouldn't drop the baby, but what do I care?

"I'm going home," I say.

"To your mad ma," she says.

"What's that supposed to mean?" I say.

"She's trying to get my ma to go to the police and say some other man hurt her in the Woody," says Dirty Alice.

"It *was* another man. My ma is right. Your ma made a big giant mistake saying it was Patrick Thompson and my da says she's too scared to tell the truth because it would make her look stupid," I say.

"My ma isn't stupid," says Dirty Alice.

"And neither is my ma," I say.

"What will happen to the man your ma says hurt her?" she asks.

"He's going to go to jail for a thousand years and so he should. I hate him."

"He won't go anywhere without my ma."

"What are you talking about?"

"I heard them talking."

"You were spying?" I say, disgusted because it is different when Dirty Alice spies.

"I wanted to know what your ma was doing in my house," says Dirty Alice.

"What else did they say?" I ask.

"My ma cried," says Dirty Alice. "And so did your ma, so don't be getting smart."

"What else?" I say.

"I don't know. It was hard to hear," she says.

I didn't even see Luke. He slapped me from behind and quite hard across the head. He's lucky I didn't slap him back but no one is to slap Luke. It's how it is.

"What did you do that for?" I say, rubbing my scalp.

"Louisa doesn't want this dragged up again. She's done with it. You understand?" says Luke.

"If the man who smokes and wears the chain doesn't go to prison, then all the women in the world are doomed forever. Even Alice," I scream.

"Don't you say stuff like that, you little bugger," says Luke.

"It wasn't Patrick Thompson, Luke. It wasn't," I say.

"Come on, Alice," says Luke but he looks upset.

"Will they let me hold Amanda?" Alice asks.

"Maybe," says Luke.

They walk off, leaving me in the Woody. It's cold and wet and so I go home, but there is no one there. I think of the pervert with the orange hair not caring about what he has done to anyone and it makes me so angry I punch the door and make a dent in it. I will get a hiding for it for sure.

forty-three

Mr. and Mrs. McFadden come to our house with baby Amanda. Mrs. McFadden rests the thing in her arms. I take a look. She's like E.T. I don't think babies are cute or anything like it. They're always wet and make stupid noises, but the grown-ups love the sight of them and everyone goes mad with excitement. Granny lifts the baby and rubs her nose. Ma tickles her tummy, but Mrs. McFadden isn't too happy about that. Mrs. McFadden doesn't look too happy about anything. Da just smiles at the baby and says, "She's a wee smasher," but really he doesn't care at all.

"Men," says Ma and laughs, but Mrs. McFadden doesn't laugh and that makes Ma go quiet again.

Mrs. McFadden is offered a seat and sits down. She is offered tea but she says no. She looks like she wants to run out the door.

"Louisa, shall we go into another room and talk by ourselves?" Ma says.

Mrs. McFadden looks at Mr. McFadden, who nods at her. She hands him baby Amanda and follows Ma out of the room.

Dirty Alice and I are sent to my room. Luke is allowed to stay with the grown-ups.

Dirty Alice has been in my room before, but it was tidy

then. Now it is all messy and all my clothes are everywhere. My toys go from one end of the room to the other. Dirty Alice pulls a face.

"Your room is a dump," she says.

"I suppose your room is all tidy and neat," I say.

"Tidier than this," she says.

Then Frankie comes in and sucks up to her. I wish he wouldn't do that, but Frankie loves everyone. There's no stopping him.

"Are they letting you hold Amanda yet?" I ask.

"Yes, but I have to sit on the sofa and not move a muscle. It's very hard, you know, because she has a very wobbly head. It's like it could fall off or something."

I laugh.

"S'not funny," she says.

"Do you want to play a game?" I ask.

"Like what?" she asks.

"Soldiers."

"All right."

And so we play soldiers and it's not a bad game at all. She is very good at soldiers and does all the noises. I still wish I was playing with one of the lads, even if she does make the explosion sounds. I have Action Men, which she loves and asks to borrow for her stupid Sindy dolls. I give her the one with no legs.

"What am I supposed to do with him?" she asks.

"I'll put trousers on him and they can act like legs. He can't stand up, but you want him for girl dolls anyway, so who cares?"

"I suppose so," she says and takes him off my hands. Now she has a husband for all her dolls. I feel bad for my Action Man.

"Do you still have your boyfriend?" I ask her.

"No," she says and then she looks away from me because she's embarrassed and so she should be. A boy has stopped liking her. It's a great shame.

"What do you care anyway?" she whispers.

This makes me go red.

"I don't," I say.

Then Luke comes in, but he knocks first because that's the kind of thing Luke does.

"We're going," he says to Alice.

"What's wrong with you?" she says because Luke is looking sulky about something.

"Ma won't testify against the man who hurt her," says Luke.

I don't know what to say.

"But why?" I ask.

"They won't believe her is why. She made a mistake before. They could say she's an unreliable witness. It could make things worse," says Luke. "Come on, Alice."

Dirty Alice grabs the broken Action Man and follows Luke out of the door.

"Thanks, Michael," she says.

She smiles at me but I don't smile at her because I don't feel like smiling at her. It's how she makes me feel.

I go to my window and watch the McFaddens go back to their house and when they're inside and have locked all the doors Mr. McFadden closes the curtains and I know it is a very sad day for their family. I wonder what Ma might have said to Mrs. McFadden.

I go downstairs.

"She's a bloody coward," I hear Da say.

"She's not a coward. She's afraid," says Ma.

"And you're not?"

"She doesn't owe me anything, Brian. She doesn't owe this family a damn thing. Everything that's been done to her is our fault and not being able to testify is our fault."

Ma throws a teacup at the wall and it's one of Granny's favorites.

"That's enough of that," says Granny.

Ma grabs for the dog's lead and storms out the door with Frankie biting at her ankles. Poor Frankie, he's always being dragged this place and that place and always when someone is running away from something.

"She's right," says Da to Granny. "This is something she will have to do on her own."

Granny gets a dustpan and brush for the broken china. "Well, isn't she the hero," says Granny.

"Shame on you, Ma," says Da and walks out the room, leaving me with Granny and her busy brush.

"What are *you* staring at?" snaps Granny. "Away to your room!"

"I've been in my room all day," I tell her.

"Then away outside and play," she says. And so I do some storming of my own and make sure to slam the door behind me.

It's cold outside but I don't care. I go straight to the Woody and when I get there I find Fat Ralph and Paul looking at nudie magazines by the tree.

"Who wants to play soccer?" I say.

"We're looking at fanny," says Paul.

"Come on," I beg.

"All right," says Fat Ralph.

"You don't want to look at tits anymore?" says Paul.

"It's boring now," says Fat Ralph. "I want to play soccer."

Paul hides the magazines inside the tree and that's when Ma pushes through the bushes with Frankie.

"What are you all up to?" says Ma, knowing fine well what we've been up to except I wasn't up to it.

"Nothing," we say together.

"Then what's that you've got?" Ma asks.

Ma goes straight to the hiding place and finds the magazines. Paul goes red and Fat Ralph runs off, giving the whole game away.

"What the hell is this?" Ma asks, waving the magazines in the air.

Paul and I say nothing. We want to run away like Fat Ralph did, but we can't. Then Ma lets go of the lead and rolls up one of the magazines and starts belting Paul with it before making a run for me.

"You dirty little bastards," she's screaming. "Dirty. Filthy. Little. Fuckers."

Paul and I make a run for it but Ma is very fast on her feet. She pulls Paul to the ground first and starts smacking him with the magazine. It's Da who pulls her away.

"Rosemary, for fuck's sake," says Da.

Poor Paul is screaming his head off and I've lost my soccer ball. People start to come out of their houses and everyone is staring at Ma, who is red with anger, her face wet with spit.

"What the fuck are you all looking at?" she yells.

It's like she's surrounded by cattle, but then Paul's ma shows up and when she sees Paul crying on the ground pointing at Ma she goes mental.

"I'll get the police on to you for this, Rosemary Murray," she cries and gathers Paul from the ground.

"He's a little pervert," screeches Ma.

"Michael looked too," says Paul.

"I did not," I say and I didn't. I wanted to play soccer.

Ma lunges for me anyway, but Da holds her back.

"That's enough," screams Da.

Ma rages at me. Her face is all twisted like she hates me more than anyone in the whole world, but the next thing she's looking around at the neighbors. They might as well be mooing at her, they're like big cows chewing cud. They can't believe what they're seeing or hearing.

"Look at you. Staring. You're all fucking perverts with your talking and your watching and your thinking. Every one of you. Perverted," she yells out.

"Come on, love," says Da and he's dragging her away. I see the McFadden curtains twitch but no one comes out of their house. Ma sees too. It slows her down a bit. She folds into Da's arms and we go back to the house. The crowd melts away. I am slow to follow my ma and my da. I wonder what will happen to me when I get home. Mostly I wonder if Ma thinks I am a pervert too. Maybe I am.

forty-four

Da's first day of work is a huge celebration. Ma makes us all a fry-up with sausages, eggs, black pudding, and potato scones. I love potato scones. They are my most favorite in the whole world. Granny pulls out a tin for Da's sandwiches and a flask for his tea. He feels like a big man all right. He puts on his work clothes and a long belt of tools around his waist. Ma goes with him to the harbor and takes Frankie with her. She is going to take a walk to the port. I have to go to school, otherwise I would go with her. I ask her if she has more studying to do, she says no, but this isn't true, though Ma hasn't looked at a book in weeks. She's very nervous because of the court case, everyone is, but we pretend not to be.

Mrs. McFadden takes her baby all over the housing estate, but she never goes far. Ma and Mrs. McFadden nod when they see each other and smile a little, but only a little, there's a line between them now. Ma can't poke her head into Mrs. McFadden's pram and Mrs. McFadden can't pat Frankie on the head or anything like that. It's small smiles and awkward nods of the head and passing by quickly. It's all that's wanted right now.

The kids in the estate are playing with me again but things are a bit boring on the weekends. The rain has been terrible and when we're at school we have to play indoors and sometimes

Mrs. Roy makes us play games I hate. She's always trying to teach us how to play chess. I like Twister, but someone always gets hurt at Twister and the game is ended. I don't know why she has it at all. I suppose I like Operation the best with the funny little man on his back with his great orange nose making a right noise when you pick pieces of his body from him, but all the parts are missing and Mrs. Roy has these tiny little bits of paper in there in place of his bones and his heart and his lungs and they're very hard to pick up with the tweezers and so you always lose.

When it rains on weekends we mostly play together at Fat Ralph's house. Fat Ralph's ma is a really nice ma. She always has good things to eat and tells me I'm a beautiful boy. She tells Paul he's a wild man. He loves that. He's stupid, that Paul.

When we are playing soldiers and I am winning, Fat Ralph says, "Michael, my ma says your ma is very brave for going to court to get the pervert man."

At first I want to punch Fat Ralph for even mentioning it but I can see how scared he is and so I'm also thinking it was a nice thing to say.

"And what does your ma think?" I ask Paul, knowing fine well what his mother thinks.

"Who cares about my ma?" he says, staring at Fat Ralph's swirly brown carpet. "I just hope they get the man that hurt Mrs. McFadden and left her in the Woody like that. He should go to jail forever and ever."

"He should have his prick cut off, that's what my ma says." We all laugh at Fat Ralph spitting the word *prick* like that.

"He should have his brains bashed in and it should be our

feet that do it. We'd bash him and bash him and bash him," says Paul.

I jump on the bed.

"I'd do kung-fu chops on him like this," I say.

"I'd saw his head off like this," says Fat Ralph and makes the noise of a chainsaw.

"I'd make you fart on his face," says Paul to Fat Ralph and that has us rolling about.

"I wish I had been in the Woody before he hurt Mrs. McFadden. I would have caught him and killed him with the biggest stick I could find." I fall to the side of the bed.

No one agrees or disagrees; we're just quiet for a bit and glad when Fat Ralph's ma brings us lemon barley water and sandwiches with chicken paste. I give Fat Ralph's ma my best smile and not for the sandwiches but for having good thoughts for my ma; she needs all the good thoughts she can get right now.

forty-five

D a wins the pools; it's not a mad amount of money but it's enough to fill Grandpa Jake's savings account again. We've been dipping into it all year.

"With all the trouble we've had it's a godsend," says Granny, who thinks God only sends good things to good people, but never mentions the things the Devil sends to good people.

"Fortune is smiling on us, Rosemary. Fortune is smiling on us." Da gives Ma a big sloppy kiss on the cheek. "You can concentrate on your studies now, love, forget the job," he says.

"I like the job," says Ma.

"Whatever you like," he says.

Da agrees with everything Ma says right now because she is nearing the court case and frightened to death to face her attacker again. I want to go with her and hold her hand. I also want to throw a punch at him, but Da says I can't.

"It's no place for children," he tells me.

"But I know all there is to know, Da. I've been listening in the kitchen for ages. I want to see him."

"Michael, there are things you can never know. There are things Ma will have to say about the attack, things she hasn't even said to me. I'm sorry, son."

"What things has she not said to you?" I ask.

"Don't, Michael." Da's face goes red.

"Fine. Don't tell me. I don't care anyway." I stomp off to the Woody. Dirty Alice is there. She's everywhere.

"Hi, Michael," she smiles.

"Hi," I say, but I'm wondering about the smile and her friendly way.

"You shouldn't come here on your own," I say. "It's dangerous for girls."

"No one would touch me," says Dirty Alice.

"How do you know?"

"He's caught now and anyway I'd have kicked his balls in for him," she says and she probably would have, but I remember Ma's face when he touched her and know it wouldn't be enough.

"Sure you would," I say.

"Your ma is going to court tomorrow," says Dirty Alice.

"What if she is?" I say.

"I'm just saying," she whispers.

She looks hurt and it makes me feel bad.

"I want to go," I say.

"Go where?" she asks.

"To the court and kill him."

"You should."

"Don't be stupid."

"It's what I would do. I'd take a kitchen knife and sneak on the ferry and get to the courthouse and stab him to death in the guts," she says.

We mull it over for a while.

"We'd end up in Juvenile Hall," I say.

"Probably. Maybe your da will do it," she says.

"Nah, he has a new job and we won some money on the pools," I tell her.

"Tell him you want to go on holiday, maybe go to Greece. It's magic in Greece," she says.

"I hate Greece," I say, thinking of her stupid boyfriend probably waiting for her on a beach with roses or something stupid like that. I remember how much I hate Dirty Alice. I give her a scowl. She turns to the spot where her ma was found.

"Why don't we go to the courthouse anyway?" Alice says. "We can sneak on the ferry and wait for him when he goes into the courtroom. I'll boot him in the nuts and then we can run away."

"What will I do?" I ask.

She has a think to herself. "Spit on him. Your germs will kill him," she says.

I don't like that much and she knows it, but then she smiles to remind me she's just joking and that makes me feel better.

"OK, I'll spit on him, you kick him in the nuts," she says.

"I don't have any money for the ferry," I tell her.

"I have enough for both of us," she says.

"You would pay for me to go on the ferry?" I ask.

"I will," she says.

"That's very nice of you, Alice." I don't say Dirty Alice. It's a very expensive boat ride.

"We'll be on the eight o'clock, your ma and da will be on the six thirty."

"What about school?" I ask.

"Fuck school. This is important."

And she's right. This is important.

forty-six

I had some money saved in my piggy bank, except it's not really a piggy bank, it's a soccer ball with a slot and it only has a pound in it.

Alice was right in the end, Ma and Da did get the six thirty and what a noise they made about it. Ma was shouting about this thing and that thing. Da was calming her down and telling her they wouldn't miss the boat and everything would be fine.

"Would you stop changing your clothes?" says Da.

"The lawyer says the jury wants to see a decent woman; I'll be standing next to a prostitute. She will look like she deserved it. I can't look like anyone except a mother, it will help us both," says Ma.

"They won't think you're a prostitute, Rosemary," says Da.

"You don't know what they'll think. None of us do," says Ma.

Eventually the door closes and I get ready for my own boat ride.

"What are you up to today?" says Granny.

"Nothing. I'm going to school," I say.

"Well, be sure to behave yourself. This is not a day for trouble," says Granny. "It's the last thing any of us need."

I nod, but I know I'm going to be in a whole heap of trouble and so is Alice.

At a quarter to eight we meet in the Woody and make our way to the ferry. We're worried someone will recognize us. It's so busy no one really notices, but just in case we decide to hide in the toilet until the boat docks at the other side.

The ferry takes a long time, especially when you're stuck in a toilet with Alice who isn't saying too much. There's only one porthole and you can hear the swishing of the waters under the boat. People knock on the door like a hundred times but there is another toilet and they use that without too much fussing. Although, one time, the other toilet gets occupied by someone who takes a right long time and annoys the other passengers, but it passes and everyone gets to go to the toilet and no one bothers Alice and me.

"My ma changed her mind," whispers Alice. "She's gone to Glasgow too."

"Is that why you're all moody?" I ask.

She nods her head. "My ma says your ma doesn't stand a chance in court on her own because she took so long telling anyone, also the other woman is a prostitute and who's going to believe someone like her? My da says no one believes prostitutes."

"Don't say that. She got hurt the same as everyone else, my ma says."

"But prostitutes sell their bodies to anyone, the pervert will just say she sold it to him, that's what Luke says. He thinks it's all a waste of time and everyone will get hurt."

"Luke is a fanny, Alice." I wonder if she'll go mad at that. He is her brother.

"I suppose so," she says.

"I think it's great and brave of your ma to testify, my ma will be pleased," I say.

"But it also might be very bad," she says.

"Why?" I say, getting annoyed.

"Luke says no one is going to believe any of them. Ma already made a mistake saying it was Patrick Thompson and your ma took ages to tell anyone. Luke says Ma's putting herself through the wringer and for no good reason. Luke says she'll get hurt and our curtains will close again with all the sadness we had before."

Alice starts to cry.

"That's not true," I tell Alice. "Luke is a smarty-pants who thinks he knows it all," I say. "But he doesn't. Not all the time."

"But he might be right."

"He might not be," I say.

Someone knocks on the door.

"What's going on in there?" comes a voice.

"Can a girl not have some peace to do her business?" Alice makes a fart sound. I almost burst my hole. The door-knocker moves on and the captain tells everyone it is docking time.

The train is a right laugh. We slag off everyone we know for being stupid and tell all kinds of stories on them. There aren't too many secrets on our island, but I don't tell Alice about Marianne and her fanny, that is a special kind of secret and I know Alice wouldn't want to hear it anyway. I don't think I'll ever tell anyone in my whole wide life.

When we get to the train station we have to ask where the Glasgow High Court is and of course it's miles away and we will have to walk, having no money for a black taxi.

It is a long journey from the station and when we get there

we see all kinds of people scattered across the steps looking nervous and smoking cigarettes. Mostly people are wearing suits, but some aren't. They must be the criminals, I think, or friends of criminals. I check my own clothes, a duffel coat and trainers, a bag for my soldiers and Granny's jam sandwiches. We think we are invisible until a policeman gives us a look because he knows we shouldn't be there and so we leave the steps and make out we are just passing by.

Eventually we come back to the steps of the court. It is a big place, Glasgow High Court, and we don't know how to get in. It feels like everyone is looking at us, wondering what terrible crime we might have committed. They don't know we are not supposed to be there, we could be going to Juvenile Hall for all they know. Alice holds my hand.

"Let's go in," she says.

"I don't know, Alice," I say. The cold is making me feel a little bit shaky and I really don't know. I think maybe we should go home, but I know Alice will balk at the idea.

"What the fuck are you doing here?" comes a voice. It's Tricia Law and with a fag in her hand.

"I've come to see the rapist," Alice shouts and people stare.

"Me too," I say, but not like Alice said it.

"Is that right?" says Tricia. "And then what?"

"I'll kick his nuts," I say.

Tricia laughs. "You won't get near him. There's two policemen and a lawyer guarding the bastard." She takes a long drag of her fag and then throws it on the ground and stubs it into the pavement.

"Your da will go spare when he sees you're here."

"I don't care," I say.

Tricia rustles in her bag and gives Alice and me some Juicy Fruit, but mostly to get herself another fag.

"Have you seen my ma?" asks Alice.

"She's testified already. She's waiting with Michael's ma. It was very brave of her to show up like that. Very brave. You must be proud of her, Alice," says Tricia.

"I am but Luke says she is fragile," says Alice.

"If that's what Luke says, then it must be true," says Tricia, smoking.

I like that she says this because it means she thinks Luke is a big know-it-all and a little bit annoying. She also thinks Mrs. McFadden is stronger than we all think. She's right because Mrs. McFadden has testified and is having tea with my ma.

"I want to know the verdict," I say.

"You do? Then you're braver than me," says Tricia, who taps nervously on her cigarette. "So you want to see him, Michael? Is that why you're here?"

"I do," I say.

"Then be patient. We'll need to go round the back," says Tricia. "We can see him when court has finished for the day. Could be a while yet."

"What does he look like?" I ask.

"He's tall, built like a brick shithouse and has red hair and a beard. He's wearing a suit, but that's probably for the trial to make him look like a respectable gentleman instead of the monster that he really is," says Tricia.

"What about Da? He must be going mad," I say.

"He's there for your ma. We don't need scenes today. You should go home."

"You said I could see him," I remind her.

"Do you think your ma wants that, Michael? Do you think either of your mas wants you to see this monster?"

I'm not sure and neither is Alice.

"Come on and we'll get you home," says Tricia.

"I want to kick his nuts," I say miserably.

"Michael, I've been in there. The lawyer kicked his arse into next week. Trust me. This man is going to prison and he'll get his nuts kicked in then."

"Do you promise?" I ask.

"I swear it," and then she gives a little puff of her cigarette and she's all nervous and so I know she isn't sure. Grown-ups get it wrong all the time; it's the reason we're there.

I get in the taxi with Alice and when we are sitting tight on our chairs I jump out the other side of the car.

"Michael, what are you doing?" screams Tricia.

"I want to see Ma's monster. I've been living with him for over a year now. He's been all over my life. He's the reason for everything. I want to look in his eye. Maybe I won't kick him in the nuts but I want to see him."

"Coming or going?" says the taxi driver and he's grumpy.

Tricia sighs and gives the taxi driver some money.

"There's a cafe inside, we'll go for a cup of tea," says Tricia. "Your parents will kill me," she says, but we don't get too far because Da appears with Ma. They don't see me at first, but then they do and it's too late.

"Michael!" shouts Ma.

I am caught.

Da looks mad as a dog.

"What the hell are you doing here?" yells Da.

Alice's ma and da appear too, but they hug her instead. I am annoyed about that. Suddenly they're all crying and Alice is holding tight to her ma.

"Let's go," says Mrs. McFadden.

Suzanne Miller and her parents swoop past us. They don't care to stop. They give Ma dirty looks and stride toward all the taxis waiting in line for all the victims and criminals to go home and have their teas.

"Good luck to you, Morag," says Da to a girl I have never seen before. Ma gives her a little hug and Da shakes her hand.

"Same to you all," she says.

I watch this girl Morag walk away. She climbs into a waiting taxi and disappears inside behind the black door.

"Was that the prostitute?" I ask.

"Her name is Morag," says Ma, annoyed.

"You should be at school, you little bugger," says Da. "How did you get here anyway?"

"I wanted to see him," I say.

Ma goes red.

"We're going, Rosemary," says Mrs. McFadden and I think maybe they will hug too, but they don't. The strangeness between them remains the same.

"Be seeing you, Brian," says Mr. McFadden. The men are more friendly.

"Bye, Michael," says Alice, all smiles and joy. She takes her da's hand. She didn't get into trouble or anything and doesn't care about kicking the rapist's nuts anymore. Stupid Dirty Alice. It was her idea to come here in the first place.

"Is he going to jail, Ma?" I ask.

"I hope so, Michael." I grab for her legs. Da smiles, but Ma doesn't.

"Can I go round the back, Da? I want to see him," I say.

"No," says Da.

"Please," I beg.

"I think I want to see him too," says Ma to Da and suddenly she is holding me by the hand and taking me to see her monster. Da grabs at her.

"Rosemary, no," says Da.

"I want to, Da," I say.

Da lets Ma go and we go round the back with Tricia Law.

We wait a long time and there is a lot of cigarette smoking. Tricia thinks it's a bad idea and so does Da. Eventually the door opens and the monster is brought outside with two policemen who seem very small next to this man. I feel bad for my ma. She could never have escaped him. His hands are like giant knots and his body as strong as a bull.

"Fucker!" yells Tricia.

Da says nothing. He moves closer to Ma, who hides under his arm. I grab at the fence that divides me from the man who raped my ma. I want him to look up and I want him to see me. I want to see his eyes, but he won't look at anyone. He is a coward and cowards can't look anyone in the eye.

"Hey, you," I shout but he still won't look at me.

A policeman pushes him into the back of the car and I know then his eyes are not mine to see. They belong to my ma, to Mrs. McFadden, and to a girl called Morag.

forty-seven

The flasher does not get sentenced to death and his head
stays on his shoulders.

"More's the pity," says Granny.

Ma shakes her head. "Three years," she says and holds tight
to Da's arm.

"It'll be a long three years. Think on that," says Da, patting
Ma's hand.

"He should have got a hundred, Ma," I say.

"Still not long enough for me," says Ma.

News of the rapist going to jail sweeps across town and Ma
and Mrs. McFadden are heroes for putting him away. It is in
the local newspaper and in the *Daily Record* and so everyone
in the whole wide world knows. My ma says to a journalist, "It
is good the demon is behind bars," and Mrs. McFadden says,
"I just want to get on with my life." The girl called Morag isn't
asked anything at all. She is the invisible woman. There is even
a sketched picture of the rapist in the paper but his head is low
and it is hard to see his face. I think the worst picture-drawer
in the world must have drawn him.

Professor Friendly sends Ma flowers but Da doesn't like
them because he didn't think to buy them himself. Ma goes
back to work and her studies again. She is still a little sad be-

cause of what has happened to her but Granny says it will pass and for real this time.

"It's over now," says Granny. "For all of us."

I wonder if Granny is right, if it really is over this time.

"But Ma was mad when he went to prison, Granny. She says he won't be in jail long enough," I say.

"Your ma will have to lump it," says Granny. "We all have to try and forget this bad thing that has happened, especially your ma."

Ma comes in and I ask her if she'll be able to forget.

"I'll try, Michael," she says.

"I'm off to play keepy-uppies," I say.

"You must be able to do a million of them by now," says Ma.

"Almost fifty," I tell her.

"Must hurt your little legs," she says.

"He's young," says Granny.

"Not as young as I would like," says Ma and starts to help Granny fold the clothes.

The doorbell rings.

"Go see who it is, Michael," says Granny.

It's Skinny Rab and he's standing in front of a lot of our neighbors.

"Go get your ma, Michael," says Skinny Rab.

"Ma!" I yell and when she comes to the door she sees what I see, a swarm of people smiling and chattering outside our door. I wonder what they want and when I look up Mrs. McFadden is standing on our doorstep with Mr. McFadden, Luke, and Alice wondering the same and as surprised as we are.

"Well done, girls," someone shouts.

People clap. "Nice one, ladies," someone else says.

Then someone whistles and there is more clapping. It's like we are on a stage and Ma and Mrs. McFadden have sung a great song together. Ma goes red. Then Da appears and he is all smiles. He puts his arms around Ma and she is so embarrassed I think she might disappear under Da's armpit. It's like everyone around me is suddenly happy and I am the best boy in the world for having a brave ma who beat her monster and had him sent to jail. Ma and Mrs. McFadden look at each other and a little wave flutters between them and I see the ice thawing.

forty-eight

Six months after the trial there is good news for Ma and Mrs. McFadden. It turns out there were three other women afraid to tell about the monster that hurt them. Ma's monster. I read in the paper that his name is Frank O'Sullivan. It is strange to read his name. No one says it out loud in our house. We call him other things but never by his real name. He gets seven years in prison and this makes Da buy champagne. He invites the McFaddens but only Mr. McFadden comes. Mrs. McFadden has to stay with baby Amanda, but she sends her best wishes and a box of shortbread for the celebration. Then Alice shows up and I have to share the shortbread with her, which I am not at all happy about, not one little bit. She says thank you like a hundred times like I have given her the Crown jewels or something.

When all the adults have finished the champagne Da pours some drinks from under the cupboard next to the flour and Mr. McFadden is well pleased. Even Ma has a drop. When Tricia Law appears with her own champagne, I know there will be a big night in the Murray household. Alice and I go up to my room because we are sent there and because it is very boring being with grown-ups who are drinking and talking about Margaret Thatcher and the IRA and all the other terrible things happening in the world, especially unemployment.

Da is very lucky to have a job at all, says Mr. McFadden, who has been unemployed since his first wife died, but he doesn't seem to mind and neither does Mrs. McFadden. I wonder if Mr. McFadden is rich and when I ask Alice she says he is because he gets a dole check almost twice a month.

"Let's go down to the Woody," says Alice.

"It's dark," I say.

"Don't be a baby," she says. "They won't even notice we're gone. It will be a laugh. Bring your soldiers and we can pretend we are at war," says Alice, going downstairs. I smell the fag smoke from the kitchen and decide Alice is right. It would be fun at the Woody. I grab a bunch of soldiers and give some to Alice and we sneak out the front door. Alice sneaks into her da's shed and gets a torch. When we get there it's like a grassy graveyard and it makes me scared. I worry about animals like snakes and rats coming out of the grass. They don't care at night and would bite your arse in a minute, but it is obvious Alice couldn't care less and so I don't say anything. We find a wee spot and have a good old game of soldiers. I win, but Alice doesn't mind. I kill all her soldiers and it's easy as pie but then it gets cold and there is nothing to do anymore. We can see the lights in my kitchen are still on and the party is in full swing. There is even music playing and I bet a million pounds my da is singing stupid songs about Scotland. Alice moves closer to me and it makes me move along a bit. I got a hiding last time Alice was close to me.

"I'm not going with the Greek lad anymore," says Alice.

"I don't care," I say and I don't.

"Yes, you do," she says and kisses me smack on the cheek. I want to wipe it clean but I don't. I kiss her back. I kiss her like I have seen in the movies and I tumble on top of her like a madman. It doesn't feel wrong, maybe because we have done it before, maybe because Alice and me know what we are doing, being so mature now.

Eventually we stop kissing and Alice wiggles from underneath me.

"You're a good kisser, Michael Murray," says Alice out of breath.

"You're good too," I say.

"I have to go home now," says Alice. She dusts herself down from the grassy Woody, which is all over us from the rolling in the grass we've been doing.

"Don't tell anyone about this," she says.

"I won't," I promise.

She smiles and skips back to her house, leaving me with all the soldiers to carry back on my own.

I go home to my house and I am very pleased with myself. Everyone is downstairs and so I take out a nudie magazine and let my willy go mad. I know it is wrong, I know my ma wouldn't like it, I know Alice's da wouldn't like it, his head would burst open, but it is what boys do when they are excited by girls and I am very excited about the beautiful Alice. Anyway, it's OK if you're on your own; Paul says it is normal and so does Fat Ralph. It's only wrong if you do it in front of girls and they can see you. You can only ever do it to yourself and for the rest of your life.

forty-nine

D a is very excited. Ma has gone to work with Tricia Law and he has something planned. Ma has had a good week and passed all her exams. She will become a teacher now after she does some more studying and Da is very proud of her, but he is also afraid.

"She's moving on, Ma," he whispers to Granny.

"She's bettering herself," says Granny.

"What if she betters herself so much a builder will not be good enough for her? She's always been the smart one," says Da.

"After what you two have been through wild horses couldn't separate you and anyone can see it. You're a strong man, Brian Murray, and I couldn't be prouder of you."

There is a little silence between them and I wonder if they are hugging. I am dying to look but I am hiding behind the door and not supposed to be listening or anything at all.

"Today of all days," he says to Granny.

Da is upset by the rain. I don't know why. I love the rain. It cleans the entire world and makes everything fresh again.

"It won't matter to Rosemary, son. She's going to go mad with joy. Where's Michael?" says Granny.

"I'm here," I say, forgetting I am not supposed to be so close to the kitchen door, but Granny hardly notices, though she scowls a little like she does know but has no time for upsets today. I wonder what is going on.

"Away upstairs and put your good clothes on," she says.

The only good clothes I have are the ones from Christmas and they include Granny's jersey, which is already too small for me. I will look stupid, I think.

When I am dressed I am called downstairs and there is *more* champagne sitting next to *more* flowers and I wonder if the monster is dead, this would be the cause for a great party and all kinds of joy and happiness.

"What's going on?" I ask.

"Something very special indeed," beams Granny.

Da enters the room with a giant box and places it on the table. He looks at his watch.

"Is it Ma's birthday?" I ask, worried I have forgotten.

"No," says Granny. "It's better than that. Much better."

"She should be here any minute now," says Da, but Ma is not any minute and eventually Da has to take a seat and grab for his paper. He rustles it about and gets irritated by everything he reads. He is totally impatient and clock-watches for ages. He is driving me mad, but so is Ma and I wish she would hurry up. The jersey I am wearing is tight and I am desperate to take it off.

"That Tricia is keeping her gabbing no doubt," says Granny, all annoyed.

Eventually the door rattles and Ma enters the kitchen all wet with Tricia Law. She sees everyone dressed to the nines, the champagne, the flowers, and the big present.

"What's the occasion?" she says.

"Open your gift," says Tricia, lighting a fag. She is soaked through and so is Ma.

"Let me take my coat off," says Ma.

"Leave it on," says Da.

"What for?" says Ma.

"Open the present and you'll see," says Da, all excited.

"Well, I hope it's an umbrella, I'm soaked through," says Ma.

"Open your gift, Rosemary," says Granny impatiently.

Ma starts to peel the wrapping off her present. About time, I think.

I am annoyed because I know it's not an umbrella; it is something everyone knows about except me. This is a door I was not standing behind when they were making this secret, I think.

Anyway, she unwraps the papers and finds it's a box with more paper on it. It's one of those big presents you have to un-wrap and unwrap until you get to a tiny box where the treasure lies. Ma takes ages and there is paper all over the floor and every time she is confronted by another box she screams and laughs. Eventually she reaches the treasure and it is a small velvet box. A ring, I think. A big diamond ring. How boring, is my next thought, but then Ma opens the box and it is not a ring, it is a key.

"What's this?" she smiles. Da hands her an envelope with papers in it.

"It's what you always wanted, a home of your own," says Da. "A view. This house to share with your family and for always." Da turns red at this. "Is that what you want, Rosemary?" He worries she will say no. Things are very different now.

Ma looks into Da's face all pink and eager for an answer and nods. She grabs for him and kisses him like I kissed Alice. I am mortified to see them like this. I look to the ground while Tricia playfully rubs at my hair.

"Juicy Fruit?" she says. I nod.

"Shall we open the door?" says Granny, even though Ma has already opened the door today and with the same key she has in her purse, but somehow this key is different. With our raincoats on and the smell of the sea drifting from the harbor we stand on our doorstep while Ma turns the lock and opens our front door. Ma steps inside her home and onto the landing. We are right behind her. We would follow Ma anywhere. Once inside Ma closes the door shut and everything feels warm; we were freezing on that step but happy to be there for Ma's sake. She is bright and cheered. She has a view bought from the government and the last thing Da wanted, but he wants Ma more. When she grabs for me I am glad. I am gladder than any boy can be. My ma loves me and with the door closed behind us we can have our party now.

Drinking champagne and having a good old time Ma finds my eyes watching her across the room. She makes a kissing motion and sends it to me in the air. I am supposed to catch it like a baby and today I think I will. It might have made me cry if I was a baby, but I am not a baby. I am the toughest lad in the estate and the toughest lad in the estate doesn't cry about anything in the whole wide world. Not one thing and not today.

Acknowledgments

When you're writing your acknowledgments it's hard to know where to start; so many people have supported and encouraged me on this very privileged road and I could hug them all. I want to make mention of the women in my family who taught me to listen and to laugh, my granny Hunt, my great-auntie Jean, my great-auntie Betty, my auntie Ginny, my auntie Betty, and my mother—strong, able, and hilarious. No one can imagine the laughs in a room full of MacDonald women, but I was assured by them all (and generally amid a cloud of smoke) that if I learned to laugh young, then life would go easy on me. They were so right.

I want to thank my hometown of Rothesay. When I left home I was told by a much older generation, "You can go, but you'll come back. Everyone does one way or another." Wise words. My pen is a pepper shaker and always spills the influence of where I come from. I am very grateful. I also want to thank Susanna Maggioni for the use of her little cottage by the river in Treviso, a writer's heaven.

To my editor, the insightful Laurie Ip Fung Chun at Windmill Books, whom I have had the privilege of working with for over two years now. We're always on the same page and the talent you lend me is received with much gratitude. I thank my agent, Alex Christofi, in the same vein.

To the hardworking team at HarperCollins I give thanks. You have supported my voice in so many ways and sent me on an incredible journey.

And finally to my grandparents, Len, Nan, Biddy, and Danny. Wish you were here. I have tons to tell you. xxx

About the Author

Lisa O'Donnell won the Orange Screenwriting Prize in 2000 for her screenplay *The Wedding Gift*. Her debut novel, *The Death of Bees*, was the winner of the 2013 Commonwealth Book Prize. She lives in Scotland.